I0764656

CURBSIDE

By

JL Walters

ISBN 978-0-9848987-2-5

Always for Ellen and the boys:

Townsend, Jackson, Aidan & Sean

One

In a dark alley on the good side of town sat a lone red Jaguar convertible, engine idling, beige top up against the night. Colorless vapor blew from the tail pipe as warm engine exhaust met chill whipping wind brought in from the coast by the mountains and deserts far inland. Drops of condensation fell from the stainless steel muffler, measuring time and accumulating on the broken asphalt. Inside the little English car Linda O'Brien, pretty, exhausted, frantic, freaking out, and held her cell phone. The one provided by her employer for their exclusive communication day and night, but mostly night. Linda O'Brien listened as the man on the other end of the line berated her. She took it all in, trying to remain calm. Trying to be the woman she knew she was. The woman her father, career Marine Sergeant Henry O'Brien raised with her five brothers to be a ball-buster. She was having trouble being herself.

She did not feel like a ball-buster. Alone except for the stream of disappointment pouring into her ear from the Hollywood Hills. As Ted Conway ranted, she considered the amount of cocaine she snorted every day, trying to decipher if it still helped her perform better at her job as it once undoubtedly had. She thought of her teen years in her father's barrack's housing and her brothers and so many men in uniform. She had had to plead to be sent away to the East Coast all-girl boarding school outside Boston just to catch up to the rest of the young women of her generation in the nineteen-seventies. Just to be more than another tomboy kicking all the other girl's and boy's asses after class in the small military-base town.

At a pause in Ted Conway's cellular abuse, Linda O'Brien interjected, "I know Ted. I know. It'll never happen again. No. No. You don't need to promote anyone else. I'm your man."

It felt to her like a scripted thing to say. Ted Conway was a scripted guy, never ad-libbing, never taking chances unless he saw three or four ways to profit from what everyone else perceived as inevitable failure.

His abuse of her, she could see him propped on one elbow laying on a massive hand-made Swedish mattress engulfed by sheets and bedding that cost more than she was paid by him in one week, his glasses on his head, his wife, still perfect after so many years of tanning beds and cosmetic surgeries; eyes, nose, chins, cheeks, ears, tits three times and each time much bigger, ass, veins, tummy, vagina after the kids, laying next to him in a Valium and vodka stupor, having just suffered his marital yearning like a dog owner training a puppy not to jump on her by remaining perfectly still until the unwanted behavior and attention passed.

"What was the point of trying to keep this job?" She wondered.

She had been valedictorian of her class at Brown. Had published fiction for years working as a lowly copy editor for First Fiction, happily living in The Village, for so many years. The call of Hollywood, the salary, the glitz, the allure of being wanted by a national show, although a daytime weekly strip, a serial, a soap opera, with little prestige to anyone other than soap opera lovers, had made her head swell.

She left New York. Married an actor, divorced the actor, and never saw her kids. Her Philippine nanny was raising them now professionally she was a pariah, unable to work for any other show, branded a soap opera talent just like the producers and directors and actors: the lowest well-paid Hollywood insiders, nearly outsiders, only one wrung above valley porn-industry regulars.

Ted Conway continued to explain to her all the ways her arcs were weak in his clipped SoCal Executive Producer's baritone as she emptied an airline bottle of booze, vodka with a comic-sounding Russian name, Vodlika, into a cardboard cup half-full of cold, brothy, drive-thru take out coffee still in the car's cup-holder from a forgotten distant morning. All mornings seemed like phenomena from another lifetime.

She stirred the coffee with a ballpoint pen she found on the floor board, licked the pin clean, clicked it a couple of times, sucked the drips from its insides, dropped it back on the floor mat, and sipped the boozy coffee. The vodka cut at her but she swallowed it, and the coffee, in one long drink, a line of brown liquid trickling dark against her skin from the corner of her mouth and wetting the little phone in her hand where she pressed it against her cheek.

Linda O'Brien swallowed, stammered, "Please don't threaten me -- please -- you can count on me Ted -- I know you took a big risk on -- no -- I won't let it happen again. You'll have all of it in the morning. Seven hours. I'll fix it -- I'll see you in seven hours. I -- Hello? Hello?"

He was gone.

"Fuck."

She hung up the phone, mashing the button harder than necessary and flipping it shut. She tossed it into the seat next to her and sighed, head back, hands on the leather steering wheel, the orange dash lights glowing into her mind through closed eyelids. She opened them and stared at the brown woven fabric above her head keeping the chill evening away from her soft spoiled skin.

"Brown is a million miles away," she thought. "I never should have come here. I hate this fucking town. I hate this stupid industry. Short fiction was better for my soul now I have to pay for private schools. Do they have private schools in Montana? Fuck. I hate Montana too. Snow and ice and old poor rednecks, and new rich yuppies. Fuck."

She took another gulp of the vodka coffee. She snorted and wiped her nose hard, then fished the little brown empty glass vial from the passenger floorboard and, with a pinky finger, swabbed the dust from the inside of it and the black plastic lid then sucked the pinky and wiped at her nose again. Mind back on track, thinking of private school tuition for little kids totaling more than her mom's Hilton Head mortgage, Linda O'Brien rifled through a black worn leather datebook and tattered slips of paper. She picked up a Blackberry, most of the button's characters worn away, and scrolled through its address book. She put it down, picked up her iPhone, and scrolled through its address book. Put it down, retrieved a Macbook from the seat next to her, scrolling through windows and addresses in her off-line email.

Eventually, she found what she was looking for, picked up her cell phone, and dialed. It rang; she looked at the clock on the corner of the glowing laptop's screen, eleven forty-five in the evening. It rang more, a woman's voice answered, tired, asleep, and afraid of bad news, or worse: of being bothered from sleep for no good reason.

Linda O'Brien failed to recognize the phone had stopped ringing, she had fallen into a reverie in the dark in her car, phone pressed to her ear pushing the back of her earring sharply into the soft scalp behind her ear.

The voice shook her latently awake, Linda O'Brien said, "Sandy, hey. It's me." Linda O'Brien began to cry, to weep, silently, "I gotta have it," she said, "I'm freaking out. Just one last time. Please."

She studied accumulating drops of dew on the windshield group together and roll down the cold glass. She watched the wind push the clouds across the sky exposing the moon for a moment behind tall shaggy Diadore branches and confessed, "He's gonna kill me."

Linda O'Brien held her breath with the realization that he could indeed kill her. He would not actually do it himself but could hire it done. Had hired it done to get out of other contracts he deemed detrimental to his life's work after the party involved disappointed him or cost too much just to buy off. It was widely known the soul reason they recruited her, all their talent, from New York. It was also why no one ever quit. At least never quit without an off the books payout. She fumbled for a pack of cigarettes, found one crushed and empty. She wadded it tighter and tossed it into an empty booster seat in the diminutive rear seat.

"He's gonna kill me," she said it again and it did not seem so fantastic hearing it a second time. Maybe she would get used to the idea. Get used to the possibility. "I don't know what else to do. I lost it. I can't get it back. He's gonna get rid of me. You know how he gets rid of people."

Linda O'Brien brightened as the woman on the other end of the phone, Sandy Folson, spoke. The night seemed a little less ominous, a little less dark to her. Sandy Folson was Linda O'Brien's knight in shining armor, again.

Linda O'Brien confirmed, "In an hour. Yes. Okay. I'll bring all I have. Yes. Bye."

She mashed the off button, let the phone fall into the passenger seat, and rested her forehead on the brown leather steering wheel. She sat up, looked around, swirled the slight remains of coffee and vodka in the bottom of the cardboard cup, tipped it to her mouth, finished the coffee chewing the few grounds left on her tongue, pressed the button that rolled the window down, threw the coffee cup out, found an stale half-pack of cigarettes in the compartment in the driver's door, lit a cigarette with a green disposable lighter, and drove away.

Around the corner, she remembered to click the car's lights back on and switched the windshield wipers into intermittent motion. The radio played a Chopin sonata and it sounded to her like a death song. Switched off, the silence of the car enveloped her. With no options left Linda O'Brien navigated dark street-light-yellowed streets, pulled the expensive little car up to a curbside bank machine. She filed through bankcards in her big designer wallet extracted off the floor from a huge designer purse. At length she picked a card, skipping over all the other closed and overdrawn accounts. The sight of the useless money market cards were like sand in her eyes, each dollar spent and gone a painful grain, an individual reminder of her slow and flailing fiscal failure. Out of the car she bee-lined to the ATM and inserted her lucky card of choice, punched in the numbers, the same numbers of her now meaningless wedding anniversary.

She thought, "what if you're only allowed the number of days of happiness in marriage as your anniversary abbreviates into a four digit PIN?"

She waited, pushed more buttons, trying to squeeze more money from the machine than there was in the account. It denied her. She aimed a little lower. She hit the mark; the wide, thin door opened and spit cash out like paper vomit from a mechanical mouth. She pried the stack of bills out of the machine, the funny cash-door shut, then reopened, and spit out more bills. She removed the card and receipt, the one now useless, the other a printed confirmation of her fatal financial anemia, and returned to her car. Inside she rummaged the detritus on the passenger floor mat and came up with a plain grease-stained brown bag from her favorite taco stand. She dumped out the old plastic fork, napkins, and baggie of wasted lemon and radish wedges, dropped the stack of money in, and pushed the bundle down between her legs under her thighs for safekeeping drove hurriedly away punching more numbers into her cell phone.

A few minutes and many midnight blocks later Linda O'Brien pulled the flashy convertible up to another dark curbside in a forgotten city suburb. Trash littered the tree-root cracked sidewalks and immobile cars decorated the municipal property. Low chain-link fences, metal screen doors, and For Rent signs with Asian contact information like Happy Golden Property LLC written on them festooned private property that was neither happy nor golden.

"This neighborhood," she thought, "matches my pathetic pecuniary position. I should just move the kids here to be closer to my kind of people."

A dark man in dark bilious clothes walked out of the shadows, approached his waiting customer. Linda O'Brien pressed the button lowering the passenger-side window, stretched and handed the man some bills extracted from the paper bag. The man in turn handed her a small baggy and slowly, deliberately, returned to the darkness, away from the curbside, as Linda O'Brien drove quickly away, feeling as always; she was risking her life not only by taking the contents of the baggie but also in their acquisition.

Linda O'Brien pulled the little car up to another curbside ATM cluster; this one afforded her the privilege of remaining in the car. She rifled the wallet; again, she skipped most of the cards, again, landed on a long shot. She pushed the button and her window lowered into the door, she inserted the card and entered the PIN of her first child's birth date.

"Why would I use such an important, non-material date for the continued access and retrieval of blood money?" She wondered to herself.

Again, she selected her ideal amount of cash. Again, it denied her. It took three more tries before she got down below the magic number, beneath the threshold of cash available to her. She looked at her watch, the perfect platinum and diamond Tag Hauer her father gave her for college graduation so many long years ago. It was just before midnight. Again, the ATM mouth opened; again, she pulled the stack of bills out and stuffed them with the others into the taco-stand paper bag. The machine produced a receipt and returned her card.

She took the card, held it in her hand. Removed the receipt; its time-stamp read 23:59:07. She looked at her watch again, then reinserted the card, entered the PIN again, requested the same amount again, and felt a rush of relief when the door miraculously opened and piled up a tall stack of cash for her, again.

"Minimum Daily Withdrawal Amount my ass," Linda O'Brien muttered as she added the bills to what now amounted to a brick of money in the taco-less taco bag. She removed the card and the receipt; its time stamp read 00:00:02.

Linda O'Brien stood at her favorite taco stand's window, La Estrella, on the sketchy Latino side of town. Florescent lights bathed the outdoor eating area in a yellow glow. The taco stand windows, painted in bright colors with menu items, kept the taco clerk and cook separated from the customers who at the moment numbered one, Linda O'Brien, alone. The cook sat on a white five-gallon bucket with a metal lid in the back of the shop near the massive gray ovens looking at a Mexican low-rider and naked-pinup girlie magazine.

Linda O'Brien, order of tacos on the counter in front of her, held a card, yet another card, out to the taco clerk, haggling through the little hole in the glass, her car parked behind her at the curbside, "Cash back. I want cash back."

She spoke slowly, knowing no Spanish. The crazy white woman bewildered the taco clerk. She was tired, her feet hurt, the strap of the apron she was required to wear was rubbing her neck raw. The cook would try to grope her again as soon as the crazy rich woman drove off in her money car.

The taco clerk said, repeated, "No cash back. No cash back."

Linda O'Brien told her, "I'll give you fifty dollars, just give me all the cash you have in the drawer and charge my card for the amount. Please?"

The taco clerk thought for a moment, she thought about fifty dollars, she thought about closing and going home and going to bed, with no more greasy onion hands rubbing her thick bra straps through her shirt if she could no longer make change, then reconsidered, "Okay."

"Okay?" Linda O'Brien asked, confirmed.

"Okay," the taco clerk said again opening the drawer with a white plastic knife wrapped in cellophane slid under the register, clicking the manual release. She counted out the bills, including the fifties and hundreds from under the dirty black plastic bill-tray insert.

"Oh my God, thank you so much!" Linda O'Brien said.

Then the taco clerk pocketed fifty, slid Linda O'Brien's platinum card through the point-of-sale card reader, and slid the receipt, the card, and all the cash back into her waiting manicured fingers through the slot in the glass on the counter.

"Wait, you give me five back. I forgot charge you the tacos," the taco clerk said.

Linda nodded, extracted a five-dollar bill, and slid it back under the partition window. The taco clerk shut the window that secured the sheet of thick clear plastic with the hole and slot, locked it, turned the OPEN sign around, and clicked off the external lights. The taco cook looked up, bewildered.

Linda stuffed the cash into her ass-less baby-boomer jean pockets and pulled the folded paper plate of tacos out of the brown paper bag. She unwrapped the aluminum foil from around the now-soggy paper plate and began to eat, standing in front of the taco stand, resting against the order counter. Mouth full, dark red sauce on her chin, she knocked on the window, interrupting the taco stand employee's heated discussion over closing, and gave them a thumbs up, chewing. They looked at her; smiled as though they cared about her good opinion, which of course they did not, and resumed their argument.

She walked past the little concrete tables and around her car, placed the plate of tacos on the convertible's brown fabric top, rummaged her massive purse for her keys. The street was deserted; all the other shops closed for as far as she could see down either side. Suddenly a dark figure was approaching her, a man stood menacingly close to her before Linda O'Brian realized.

"Gimme your purse, bitch!" The mugger demanded. Linda O'Brien's purse contained the brown paper bag with over ten thousand dollars in it.

"I'll be God-damned," she thought rummaging for her keys, "if any skulking crack-head motherfucker is gonna take this away from me, away from my babies, away from our future."

When she found what she was looking for she stopped in mid chew and, turning toward the tall faceless man in the dark hooded sweatshirt, pulled out her keys, pepper spray lid removed, and streamed a shot the same color as the sauce dribbled on her chin into the man's recessed, shrouded, face.

He yelled, clutched at his eyes and turned back the way he came, running and scratching at his eyes, crying and moaning and bumping into parked cars and disappearing back into the shadows of the barrio alley between a furniture store and used clothing store, both dark and long-closed for the night.

Linda O'Brien called after him, taking the plate in hand and getting another big bite, "Not tonight motherfucker! Not tonight!"

She unlocked the door, placed the taco plate on the leather dash and got in, purse clutched to her chest. She closed the door, inserted the key, threw the car in gear, and launched it down the quiet street.

Linda O'Brien navigated barrio streets to the ghetto grocery store. Pulling into the parking lot, she steered in large circles, thumping over the useless speed bumps and stopped beside a curbed planter full of dry, dead, brown shrubs encircling a large light pole with one large light lit, the other hanging open like a big drunk hand puppet. She sat in the stationary car surrounded by the still night, thankful to be alive and fed and momentarily liquid enough to buy momentary relief and momentary freedom.

"Maybe snooty university education isn't about being taught to do what you do," she thought as she looked around for the little baggie, "maybe it's about learning to improvise when you're no longer able, or have grown to hate, what you were taught to do."

She removed the vial from the baggie, unscrewed the little cap, licked and stuck her little finger in the small jar and then swabbed the finger up each flared nostril. Then she recapped the vial and hid it up under the passenger seat in an abandoned paper French fry cup.

Linda O'Brien looked at her watch, looked at her iPhone clock, looked at her Blackberry clock, looked at her cell phone clock, looked at her Macbook clock, and squinted at the clock nested into the dashboard of the car. They all confirmed she was on time. Plastic grocery bags, dead leaves, and yellow paper food wrappers blew across the empty parking lot. They briefly swirled in a small vortex near the wall of the distant grocery store. She pressed the button and rolled her window down a few inches, shook a cigarette out of the half pack, put it between her red lips and lit it. She inhaled the toxic smoke deeply, and then exhaled noisily.

She remembered she had gone into the big store one time to buy cigarettes. The entire place smelled to her like rotting meat. The shelves were mostly empty, what products they did carry she had not recognized and she could not read their Spanish labels. Small children in rickety metal shopping carts pushed by tired parents with books of food stamps in their hands had stared at her, as though she was a dignitary from a first-world country shopping with the third-world citizenry at the native store instead of the diplomat's grocery store, the one for the rich foreign people.

Five Latino boys, young men, on BMX bikes spray-painted dull black, rode into the parking lot. They eyed her from beneath bandanas pulled low, approached the lone expensive car in the middle of the parking lot with the stoned, pale, middle-aged woman sitting at the wheel listening to Phillip Glass. She eyed them and wondered how much pretty handguns cost. Shiny silver ones with black leather holsters, small enough to fit in a glove compartment or a purse. The boys passed, rode on, circled, and returned. Linda O'Brien popped the half-smoked cigarette out the gap in the window and pushed the button. The window rolled all the way, as one of the cyclists said something to her she could not hear or understand.

A dark Suburban with blaring headlights pulled into the parking lot, approached from the other direction, running the biker kids off. Both cars rolled their windows down. Linda O'Brien handed the paper bag full of cash up to the woman in the Suburban, Sandy Folson, wearing a purple nightgown. Sandy Folson handed a small white paper bag down to Linda O'Brien. Having barely stopped, no words exchanged, the Suburban drove quickly away.

Linda O'Brien watched in her rearview mirror as the massive SUV's rear red lights left the abandoned parking lot. She contemplated the bag in her hands. Her career flashed before her eyes; school, New York, Los Angeles, marriage, kids, divorce, the emptiness inside her when she tried to work. It all lead to this disappointing state of her life.

"Everyone else's soul is mortgaged in Los Angeles," she thought as she opened the crinkly bag and found the zip lock baggie, "why not mine?"

She peeled it open, extracted the USB thumb drive, removed its cap, inserted the funny silver connector into the corresponding hole on the side of her Macbook, clicked the mounted drive, clicked the lone document, it opened her writing application and she began to read the words on the page on the screen. It was instantly brilliant in her mind's eye. A few grammar mistakes and a couple of formatting changes and no one would know she bought it off the script market. She fumbled around and lit another cigarette, taking the poison in deeply, as she read windows up, shielding her self-inflicted menace from the world outside.

Eight blissful weeks later Linda O'Brien sat in her pristine home office, bathed in morning light from sash windows, crammed bookshelves surrounding her massive old craftsman mahogany desk. She was lost in reverie, again, staring at her new shiny Daytime Emmy. The dress she had worn, bought just for the occasion from an expensive appointment-only Santa Monica designer, hung in the garment bag on the back of the half-closed office door. It cost more than she paid for the award-winning original story and arcs that crazy night in her car, trying to unravel her career. The fantastically expensive high-heeled shoes she wore to the ceremony sat on the bookshelf, next to the gilt statue, she would not wear them again, she told herself, until the next awards ceremony and gala.

She had known Sandy Folson at Brown. She was valedictorian and editor of The Indy - The College Hill Independent - student paper, a few years before Linda O'Brien she had a stellar career writing for an international news broadcast network in Atlanta. Then something happened. Her father passed away? Her mom contracted cancer? Linda O'Brien could not remember what, exactly. Something ignited Sandy Folson's crisis-of-self prompted her disappearance, professionally, for a while.

Then she started to emerge again as a ghostwriter. Then further off-radar, as a graywriter; an uncredited, well-paid, illegal author. Her largest success in fiction that Linda O'Brien knew of was for a famous nineteen-seventy New York fiction writer's return book published in the nineteen-eighties. Her other credits, that Linda O'Brien believed, were as the graywriter for the day-to-day speeches for one of the United State's presidents in the nineteen-eighties. His speech writer ran out of ideas early on, hit an existential professional crisis, and rather than resign or lobby to be head writer, more of an editor, had turned to Sandy Folson, and edited her work then handed it in as his own. They paid Sandy Folson for the work, but more than that, they paid her to keep her mouth shut. She no longer needed an agent, a manager, a publisher, or a Rolodex full of lawyers she maintained her privacy. Sandy Folson obtained real, tangible, enviable success: well paid, internationally influential, and invisibly uncredited.

Linda O'Brien knew Sandy Folson's graywriting had won an Oscar for Best Original Screenplay, a Tony Award for Best Book for a Musical, at least one Pulitzer Prize, multiple Emmy's, and now a Daytime Emmy. Perhaps a Nobel would be forthcoming, depending on word of mouth among blocked, notable, international authors and poets.

Two

People bustled, phones rang, and conversation overflowed from offices and mixed in the active corridor dividing administrative offices from administrative assistant's cubicles. In a posh Santa Monica office building on the top floor, lording over talent agencies, publicity offices, and production facilities, the hallowed halls of Conway Productions, the nation's oldest family-owned and most respected television production company was circling wagons, battening hatches, calling in favors, and laying in supplies for a battle of ratings the like they never endured before.

The king of Conway Productions, Ted Conway, returned from Asia, Australia and India where he setting up a new year distribution deals with broadcast partners around the globe following MIPCOM, the week of international television marketing programs at Cannes before the film festival, to find that the lieutenants left in charge of his baby, his money maker, his golden goose, had in one month destroyed every quality story arc he left intact. He was receiving daily threats from the network executives in Burbank and New York, specifically from the new piss-ant Head of Network, to bump the numbers up a few points or the show could be bumped off the coveted daytime air over to cable, or worse.

In his palatial office, half the entire top floor of the building, larger than most of his employee's homes, Ted Conway, tan, graying, in a perfect dark wool Italian suit, collar open, jacket hanging over an empty leather club chair, sat surrounded, flanked, by his key employees: Mark Ellison, his right-hand man, golf partner, food runner, all round Yes Man. Burt Felton, the attorney of his parents, a successful entertainment lawyer with one client, the show, for over forty years. Grant Mallory, gray haired, muscular, gay business manager, paid to say "no" and to take question with everyone else in the room. Ted Conway perpetually fired in passion, and rehired with more responsibilities and salary when time or circumstances eventually, inevitably, proved his dissention to have been correct. The other production executives sat or stood, pleased for the moment to be witnesses instead of the focus of Ted Conway's pedantic fury.

Each paid large sums of money to agree with him, so they did. Across from this battalion of Television Production, separated by a large coffee table with a massive sundial mounted in it, a reproduction of the show's trademark sundial, seated on an ocean liner of a couch, was Linda O'Brien, looking professional in a gray suit. Next to her was the always sweating, rotund, smelly, bespectacled, chain-smoking head writer, an uncomfortable fat man, biting his fingernails, Harvey Teach: today's newest reason for the sinking of Ted Conway's show.

"Fifty-five fucking years and you're killing it!" Ted Conway fumed and because he was a billionaire and had a track record of charm and brilliance in every decision he made he took no pains to be nice.

Or professional.

Or calm.

He ranted, reciting the speech they all knew, everyone but Linda O'Brien, by rote, "From burlesque to radio. From radio to television. From black-n-white to color. From analog to digital high fucking definition. To - now - and you're strangling it! Doing what no one else has been able to do since before either of, any of us in this room, was born!"

Ted Conway glared at the shattered fat man, once a brilliant play-write, the toast of Broadway and London thought of his cardiologist, his minister, his life insurance and the three money-grubbing ex-wives waiting to fuck and suck their dial-a-boyfriends raw on sheets bought from payouts from his life insurance, and calmed himself, just a bit.

"Get out. I don't care what the fucking contract says - just have your damned agent call my lawyers so they can remove your lecherous fangs from the carcass of this now nearly bloodless show."

Harvey Teach rose slowly, winded, heavily, off the couch, it moaned as he removed his bulk from its fabric and cushion-covered frame. Ted Conway signaled silently to Mark Ellison who nodded slightly. The big man was weeping, silently; his entire massive existence was moist. Linda O'Brien was the only spectator who noted the nearly invisible exchange between the Executive Producer and his second-in-command and her stomach instantly knotted. The huge, fired writer made his lumbering way to the huge, wooden double doors and left the office.

Linda O'Brien stood to follow, was told to stay, "Not you. Sit down. You're head writer now. An Emmy goes a long way in this town. Give us more dyke boxer stories. More broads kissing. More fights. That arc is saving the show. We're bringing it back to the front. It's all worked out, we have one week of dog shit already out, but as of today we're back to your dyke prize fighters so go back to the writer's wing and assemble your crew, fire anyone you hate or think is dead weight, and get me a month's worth of booked scripts. We're all depending on you. Congratulations."

He grinned a mechanical grin at her.

Linda O'Brien was elated, "I won't let you down!"

Ted Conway interrupted her, motioned her to take her seat again and to hold on the handshake, "Yes, you will. In a year, you'll have written thirteen-thousand pages for me that I liked, we produced, and some fifty-thousand more pages I rejected you'll hate me. Hate T.V. Hate L.A. You'll want to move to Montana to raise burrow owls or some shit. If you don't already want to, that is."

Linda O'Brien insisted, "You won't regret it!"

Her schoolgirl Pollyanna enthusiasm seemed out of place even to her.

"Are you my man?" He asked her, reminding her of their late night phone conversations.

"He's a crafty fucker," Linda O'Brien thought as she reassured him emphatically, "I am."

"You have to decide," he turned to his lackeys, "You've all heard this before so start thinking of new ways to make me money with the content we already own. I want my own Broadway musical based on the show too," he turned back to Linda O'Brien, "You have to decide if you are a source of light or if you are a mirror."

She looked at him deeply, as he did her, for a sign of a clue on his serious poker face. She felt as she had when she visited her dying, dementia-riddled, great grandmother in the hospital, trying to puzzle out meaning from exasperating babble and riddles. , she managed, "Ted?"

He grinned, it was his role in life to give stock tips so complex, so brilliant, to novices, that the uninitiated had no idea they were being exposed to fiscal Grace, "There are two kinds of people on this earth. There are the folks who have original ideas, have beauty and intellect within them that makes them the flowers on the vines. Then there are the other people who do not, and spend their lives, their careers, as the vines and the bees and the soil. There are folks who create and produce light, and then there are folks who watch the light or reflect the light. I make light. These people, the whole building, reflect my light to the rest of the world where they watch the light."

She had no idea what to say.

He leaned in closer, "The sun makes the light. The moon reflects it. All the planets reflect the sun's light. They are all magnificent. The sun makes the light. Same here: I am the sun. Everyone else is revolving around me. There are spectators and there are players. In any given industry or discipline, there are never more than twenty or thirty original thinkers alive at one time, men and women who create light, who are, to turn a biblical phrase, with-the-people but not of-the-people. They create the rest produce and distribute. Both are essential."

He looked at her, smiled, said, "But you have to decide which you are and then be it. Say a man discovers something in math for the first time and then he invents a code, places that code on a small computer chip, and then teaches other folks to mass-produce it they start a new industry manufacturing cellular telephones. Soon the world transforms. Lives transform. Babies are born differently. People die less often. Lonely folks feel less lonely millions have new sources of employment. From manufacturing handsets to gluing fake gems on the handsets at shopping-mall kiosks. They all reflect the original man's light. They all reflect his light around to each other."

He steepled his fingers then gestured around, "Most of these people behind me reflect my light away to the rest of the company. Two of them are here to reflect it back onto me; makes me feel good to have them kissing my ass all day long. Reminds me that everyone can be bought, humiliated, owned, and discarded."

He grinned. She felt icy, mute.

"Erich Fromm said the same thing about love. Said, wrote, that mature love accepts wholly, embraces the original. That immature love reflects its object back. Reflects only what each person values in the other. Original ideas and reflected homage to those ideas build worlds. More or less."

He looked at the massive watch on his wrist, stood, asked, "Mark, what are we doing tonight, this evening?"

Mark Ellison extracted his Palm Pilot, scrolled, read, "Uh, we have two hours until dinner, Ted. Then you have to go to that reception at the network. Then the first fight is at midnight."

Ted Conway stood, Linda O'Brien stood too, and she suspected he was a bit crazy, maybe senile, but he was the boss.

He directed her to the far end of the office and through the large wooden doors that opened automatically, as though through magic, as they approached. The group followed Ted Conway and Linda O'Brien as they threaded past receptionists, well-wishers, office boys, and accountants.

As he guided her to his private stairway, he told her, "I never take elevators. They're too damned lazy. Makes me crazy people make money selling stair simulators, steppers, for exercise," he thumbed behind himself, "Plus I don't want to get trapped with people who work for me in a small space."

They entered the stairwell, descended rapidly.

"I had been hoping for a writer's strike. Writers are all crazy you know. Unshowered in their pajamas and bathrobes all day. Sitting, drinking, writing, and doing drugs. No offence. I had all my contacts on the board of the WGA trying to get a strike going so I could clean house. This dip in ratings has given me the push I needed so were turning everyone out above a certain salary level. New directors, new producers, new line producers, new executive producers, new show runners, new editors; everyone I can get rid of to bring in new young talent you're part of that. Part of our future. Until you burn out too. Bribing WGA officials is a lot more expensive than buying out contracts; WGA people all pretend they have a conscience; the price for what I wanted was too high. This ratings dip will be better for the show's budget in the end too. Honestly: I try to stay focused on the present and future over-seas markets. For capital and investment."

Out of the building into a pristine, cool west-side beach-coast day, they walked down a Santa Monica sidewalk, trailed by Ted Conway's mob.

They walked and Ted Conway talked, manic, he used his hands, "Now you need to understand this show is more than the longest running drama in the history of T.V. and entertainment. It's more than a T.V. show, a family, an institution, or whatever it's more than entertainment for the unemployed viewers, the shut-ins, lonely hearts, obese people, and state prisoners: this show is the livelihood and pension source of over a thousand people their families: four thousand people depend on this show, this production company, for food, shelter, clothing, school tuition, cars, and their retired parent's mortgages. This show is jobs."

The folks following them nodded in agreement, Ted Conway went on, "and I know the entire I.Q. of the people on this planet would raise at least one entire digit if we were off the air. I also know four thousand people or more depend upon this institution for health insurance, life insurance, retirement, dental care, and glasses for their little babies, and multiple ex-wives, and ex-husbands when you think of the advertisers who pay for it all, not to mention the network, who sells their goods to the viewers, the factories where they make the soap and shampoo and diapers, the unions that represent the workers and their families, the management teams, the share-holders, and their families. It spirals out. It touches many people. I know the show itself seems silly. Is silly. Believe me, I inherited this menagerie, this museum of entertainment, from my mother, and did not want it. Did not want to be the curator. I wanted to be a rock-n-roller. It turns out; this is a pretty important institution, to a lot of fine people turns a massive profit!"

Linda O'Brien, speechless, off her guard, told him, "I won't fuck it up."

Ted Conway looked into her eyes, deep into her eyes, a city bus drove by, and he waited for its massive diesel reverberations to pass, he imparted more to her than his words, said, "I know, because I won't let you."

Again, she felt icy.

They turned and faced an unmarked windowless building's side entrance. One of the followers slid his key-card through a recessed slot, and a glass door buzzed. Inside, a uniformed rent-a-cop sat on a stool reading a racing form. He nodded to Ted Conway, ignored the rest.

Ted Conway asked, "Rudy how's Bella?"

Rudy the guard answered, "Fine Mister Conway, she's just fine."

They passed through another door and were in a carpeted passage two feet wide that inclined above raised floors filled with wires and cables from the massive sound-stages just on the other side of the wall. They passed sound booths and edit bays, production booths like NASA command centers, and teams of television production workers churning out content for the waiting world. The employees smiled and looked shy or murmured quiet hellos to the mob headed by Ted Conway. Or they looked surprised, baffled at the mass of suits they had never seen before. As the entourage passed, the uninitiated gawked at their boss who had just entered their realm. It only happened once or twice a year, strictly on special occasions.

From the skinny-carpeted hall, the group turned down a massive hall lined with costumed-actors and production assistants, make-up artists and wardrobe workers following actors with last minute changes. Through a door marked QUIET DO NOT ENTER Ted Conway lead the group, below a bare bright red light bulb above another sign reading SOUND STAGE DO NOT ENTER WHEN LIT.

The posted stage managers said nothing. The group made a ruckus as they walked past the wall of ropes leading up to the forest of light-bars far over head, onto the set as actors were reciting lines, boom operators were swinging massive microphones and camera men worked dollies or followed the staged action with cameras poised on their shoulders.

Off the set crews of men and women who looked like Hell's Angels moved equipment. More actors waited for their cues, others were finding their places on set but off-camera, and alternate directors conferred, smoked, and drank coffee. Extras helped themselves to tacos from a massive catering table lorded over by a proud, handsome, craft-services chef.

At Ted Conway's entrance into the action, under the bright lights, a director yelled, "Cut!" And began to cuss as an assistant director hastily clapped a black and white speed-board with red digital numbers in front of the cameras. As Ted Conway pushed the youth out of his way the director steamed, "What the fuck are you - oh shit - hey Ted, Mister Conway, how are you today?"

Immediately the actors fell upon Ted Conway, the crew backed away, and the above-the-line talent, the on-set directors, assistant directors, and the producers from the distant booths, surrounded the venerable old bastard, quickly shaking his hand and kissing his ass, jockeying for attention.

"Okay now, I didn't come over here to interrupt your work. Lord knows we have a schedule to maintain, and at over a million dollars a production day I don't need to derail all your good hard work."

They all watched him; he told the line producer, "Get everyone in here. Now."

The line producer, an old Broadway stage director gone soft from his easy life sitting in a dark booth for fifteen hours a day reviewing the script and watching for filmed flaws, spoke into his Walkie Talkie, then his assistant rang out over the building's intercom; "All personnel to stage three. All personnel to stage three for five minutes with the executive producer, Mister Ted Conway."

In fifteen seconds, every door opened into the massive stage area and people stood gawking at the circle of suits so unfamiliar to them all. The lights came up and suddenly the crew looked out of place. The suits looked out of place.

But the man who grew up there, had hung lights with the grips and gaffers as a boy, had spied on the naked actresses changing in wardrobe, had lost his virginity to an older extra with massive fake breasts in a prop room below the stages, the entire basement filled with steam pipes and asbestos boilers, who had never had a haircut in his life except in the makeup room across the hall, until he left for college, was the only person in his natural element.

He was the only person in a room of a few hundred not affecting to appear at ease. He raised a hand and their murmuring stopped. He cleared his throat, feeling more at in charge than at any other time during his long workday.

"Friends, we are in a time of change. The show is healthy but I am taking steps to assure all our futures every day. To that end I want to take a moment to introduce our new head writer, the lovely and talented Linda O'Brien."

There was a smattering of obligatory, awkward applause, it started small with Ted Conway's army of Executive's In Charge Of Production and Studio Representatives, then spread through the entire assembly, without enthusiasm. They were a group used to lies they knew Ted Conway was lying about the health of the show, or he would not be there with them. Linda O'Brien smiled, awkward, feeling suddenly shy although not a shy person. There was a pause and she wondered if she was supposed to say something. She opened her mouth but a steady mechanical buzz filled the air and everyone streamed back to his or her places off the stage, off the set, away from the scene.

She kept smiling, unsure where to go, as the cast and crew, above and below the line, resumed their tasks and the assistant directors again tried to bring order to the interrupted scene. Linda O'Brien looked around, Ted Conway was gone, his staff was gone, and she was alone, surrounded by the people whose job was to capture her staff's ideas into digital reality. To follow her blue print to build the show. She was in their way.

The moment she left the sound-stage and entered the massive hall she was surrounded, beset upon by the staff unneeded in the take; assistant make-up artists pitching ideas at her, script monitors pushing pages of their ideas into her hands, actors and actresses with no roles in the current take lobbying for more scenes and more lines and more arcs for their characters. Linda O'Brien could not take a step in the bustling hallway. The show's unoccupied pundits and actors crushed her.

Three

Downtown Los Angeles grew through wave upon wave of boom and bust industrial cycles. The tall skyscrapers lorded over streets that did not change; they were perpetually gritty, peopled by the lonely and the over-worked. Below the tall buildings, within their foundations were the remnants of other buildings, built on top of as technology allowed, and within a few were massive arenas, lost from the maps of the historic tours, accessed from street-level by multiple buildings within the same blocks sharing common foundations.

These subterranean amphitheaters were forgotten remnants left from a time when bare-knuckle prize fighting was the sport of rich men with stables of fighters backing entire syndicates built around the wagers of fists on broken teeth.

Luckily, the American entrepreneurial spirit was alive and well, as was the American thirst for spectacle, the long shot, and blood. It was within the confines of the once abandoned arena she heard the crowd.

Samantha "Curbside" Lucas, twenty years old, head shaved found her spying through a gap in the dark curtain, down a crowded aisle, at the distant canvas ring. Home was far away on the other side of town. The white square loomed above the crowd seated close and struck an unusual contrast of white square against dark circle of spectators. It sent her heart into her throat with excitement and bliss. She flung the curtain back and pumped her fists, danced, shadowboxed her way out of the dark into the follow-spot from above, into the deafening roar of her fans. She entered the boxing arena to the crush of the crowd.

It was smoky and stank of the hard laborers standing in their seats, the throng surging with excitement and anticipation. She wore boxing gear: green and silver shorts, a silver sports tank top, tall lace-up black boots, and had her hands bound in white, zinc oxide tape. No gloves. She wore no robe, and her mouthpiece was black. The glitz of pay-per-view boxing was absent. The arena stank; the fans were a mix of immigrants, blue-collar brawlers, and wealthy gamblers at ringside. They expected blood; the canvas bore bleach-smeared stains from months of fights.

Samantha Lucas showboated her way past her jeering detractors and her cheering fans seated on either side of the aisle; racial lines drawn, she represented the non-Latino enthusiasms of the crowd. Irish punk rock ground into the crowd from the ringside loud speakers as she approached, took the stairs, and bent through a gap in the four thick bracing cables she hoped to avoid throughout the bout.

As she paraded along the ring's perimeter, soaking the crowd into every crevasse of her soul, the loud, modern, Irish music faded and a screaming mariachi tune took its place. The crowd's attention and their booing turned to the other side of the cramped arena as Esmeralda "Taco" Ortiz entered through another curtain thrown wide and paraded down the alternate aisle, the Latino side of the crowd hooting and calling to her. Her long black hair pulled back, and tied so tight, Samantha Lucas barely recognized the woman she spent the night with, bought breakfast for, and trained with all that day.

Esmeralda Ortiz danced down the aisle; she wore blue and red silks and a blue athletic top. Her hands, she wore no gloves, were taped with red, white, and blue zinc oxide tape, her mouth guard was blue, and she wore ox-blood boxing boots with blue and white laces. She approached ring-side, climbed a different set of stairs, entered the ring through the bracing cables; the women shadowed and spared on opposite sides of the ring, the entire arena on its feet as the mariachi's faded and thumping rap music now pounded the air. A short, bald, rounding man, Mills Neumann, in white button-down shirt, gold cuff links, black bow tie, black slacks, and shiny black shoes entered the ring with the women. He stood in the center of the canvas with a small once-white megaphone clutched in his hand. He motioned to the sideline D.J, the level of the pounding music slowly dropped, and the crowd sat again.

"Ladies and gentlemen," Mills Neumann, the official referee for the evening cried through his little megaphone, "the main event!"

Again, the crowd roared and was on its feet, the music resumed thumping, the women swung on the bracing cables, pumping the crowd up. The music faded again, the crowd took their seats. Money, like paper fans, counted out and exchanged, filled the balled fists of spectators wagering with their neighbors.

Mills Neumann held the megaphone to his mouth and gestured to the dark-haired woman doing jumping-jacks, "In this corner, weighing in at one-hundred-ten-pounds, in red and blue and white; the challenger, with a record of seven-and-one-and-one with four kay-oh's: Es-mer-el-da-"Ta-co"-Or-tiz!"

The mariachi music resumed with a shrill trumpet and a long call from the mariachi singer's voice, the crowd exploded in boos and hoots. Esmeralda Ortiz shadowed to the rhythm of the music. As the crowd settled, the contenders traded the briefest of looks.

The music faded, Mills Neumann continued, "And in this corner, weighing in at one-hundred-nine-pounds, in green and silver; the undefeated champion of this women's flyweight class, with a record of ten-and-oh with six kay-oh's: Sa-man-tha-"Curb-side"-Lu-cas!" The Irish punk rock resumed, with a thrashing guitar and shrill fiddle, the crowd again exploded into boos and hoots.

Samantha Lucas danced, she ran in place, as she show-boated she studied the crowd and found her bosses, the two pasty men in brown suit jackets who ran all the action, sitting, smoking cigars, trading a small half-pint of brown liquor and taking turns talking into each other's ear, smiling. The music faded the bell ding-ding-dinged, the crowd sat again, and the fighters came together with the official in the center of the ring.

Mills Neumann felt and gave an obligatory inspection of the zinc oxide taped hands of each woman, kept a hold of them as he said, "You both know the rules; I don't need a clean fight: just a good fight. Bump fists and come out swinging."

Taped fists bumped with dramatic animosity the three receded, the women returned to their corners and at the ding of the ring-side bell returned to the center of the ring, each leading her fists in front of her, looking for an opportunity to land more than just a glancing blow. Samantha Lucas was a lefty and she found Esmeralda Ortiz's right side easily infiltrated, landing a hard series of body blows against the other woman's ribs, pushing her back upon the ropes early in round one.

The first one hundred-twenty seconds passed with the women deciphering each other's rhythms and testing the other's defenses. At the ding, they receded again to their corners, where water bottles squirted into their open mouths, held by their trainers; unenthusiastic men with stables of underground fighters all working for the same bosses.

The round card model, a tan Asian woman with black hair to the middle of her back, black stiletto heels, wearing a thong-and-string shiny-blue bikini, and a diamond dangling from her flat belly walked two circles in the ring with a white placard bearing a large black number two over her head. The ring girl's raised arms stretched the already tight bikini even tighter across her massive breasts and pressing nipples. The rowdy arena watched, hooted, and whistled as she swung the card around and then left the canvas through the parted bracing cables with a firm hand on her trim waist from the helpful, smiling official.

The bell dinged at the end of the sixty-second break and the fighters resumed throwing punches against each other's raised forearms, landing only a few blows, teasing the crowd. On points, Samantha Lucas was winning; she landed more punches than Esmeralda Ortiz even managed to throw.

Samantha Lucas was a golden girl with a huge legitimate career ahead of her this illegal, bare-fisted fight would be one of her last. Her contract was ending and the men who owned her career were willing to allow her more exposure in the legitimate world of professional women's boxing.

The fighters clinched and held each other tight as they landed blows, punching their way out of it repeatedly throughout the second round. The bell dinged, they again regained their separate corners for water. Sixty seconds and a different ring model later they returned to the center of the ring at the ding where Samantha Lucas landed a rocketed, unexpected, overhand left against Esmeralda Ortiz's defenseless right temple dropping the black haired brawler like a brick, spinning and landing with all her weight on the sweat-splattered canvas with her face. The referee and the spectators in the first row heard a crack.

Mills Neumann brushed "Curbside" Lucas back to her corner and counted over the limp "Taco" Ortiz, reaching eight, and helping the stymied woman to an elbow, as the lights and the roar of the crowd washed over her confused, bruised head. Her hair had come loose, it fell into her mouth as the ring physician, and the referee helped the beaten woman to her feet. Blood dripped from her mouth and there was a small saliva-and-blood pool on the canvas mat. The crowd booed and cheered, Samantha Lucas paraded the perimeter of the ring wild with excitement and elated by her win. The referee left Esmeralda Ortiz in the doctor's care, pulling her eye-lids apart, looking at her pupils, and took Samantha Lucas by her left wrist, making her wince, as he held her arm up officially declaring her decisive victory. One bout closer to freedom.

Deep in the dark concrete corridors of the little arena Samantha Lucas, wearing a tracksuit hastily pulled on over her gear, sat on the training table in her tiny dressing room, and unwound the dirtied white tape from her wrists by the light of the single hanging bulb. Her left still hurt a lot. She sat alone, staring at her swollen black and blue meat hook of a left hand, cradling it like an unexpected newborn baby abandoned at the local fire station. A knock at the tired wooden door and Esmeralda Ortiz entered, showered and clean, dressed to go home, holding a bag of ice to her bruised temple.

"That really hurt," she said getting closer to Samantha Lucas, "how long was I out?" Then she noticed the blackening wrist and asked, "Oh baby, are you okay?"

She took Samantha Lucas' wrist gently, looked at it, kissed it delicately, and gingerly rested her bag of ice on the darkening skin.

Samantha Lucas flinched, "Me? Yeah, I'm okay. Are you okay? Eight seconds. Maybe longer. Did I hurt you bad?"

She brushed Esmeralda Ortiz's hair away, kissed her bruised temple, they held each other, and then kissed gently, deeply, for a long time. They stopped kissing and Samantha Lucas said, "I gotta get to a hospital. Can you give me a ride? I can't let the boys see my wrist."

Collecting their things in gym bags, car keys in hand, Esmeralda Ortiz said, "Of course, I'm parked around the corner."

There was one knock at the door and the two beefy men from ringside entered.

Eddie Holleran, the shorter of the two, grinned, said, "Here's our girls. Wow!" He shook his head, stopped smiling, and asked, menacingly, "I just want to know; you two call that a fucking fight?"

He stared at them for a breath then continued, "Maybe in a sorority house, or a girl's high-school locker room, somewhere, someone might call that a fucking fight, but our receipts are down and, I think I know why." He chucked Esmeralda Ortiz playfully on the chin, and confided to her, "You haven't got what it takes."

He stared at her, Esmeralda Ortiz stammered, "She caught me on the temple, I was unprepared. I can do better!"

Samantha Lucas started to protest too, and then the two men spied her blue and yellow wrist.

"Holy shit," Eddie Holleran said, "Is that broken?"

Samantha Lucas lied, "Naw, I can barely feel it. Just bruised from catching her skull more than I should've."

The two boxing promoters looked at her dubiously, Bobby McGarry, the silent partner until now, took her by the arm, examined her wrist closely, looked at her and confided "Sweetie, we traffic in a certain amount of broken bones, and have seen a lot of broken hands, and that looks broken to me."

He poked her blue wrist firmly to prove his point and she jumped in spite of herself.

Bobby McGarry turned back to Esmeralda Ortiz, "God dammit! You stupid spic bitch! You broke her fuckin' hand with your hard dyke head!"

He swatted Esmeralda Ortiz hard on her bruised temple and she fell, again, in agony, to her hands and knees seeing stars in the little room. Eddie Holleran yelled at her on the ground, "What did we tell you before the fight? She's our best earner, the best looking and most talented girl we have. She was going pro after this weekend. No one came to see you; they came to see her kick your beaner ass!"

He kicked Esmeralda Ortiz's arms out from under her. As he did, Samantha Lucas hit him in his shoulder blades with her unbruised right fist. Eddie Holleran stopped, turned, looked at her as if she blew a feather at him, and laughed, "What the fuck? You hit me. You think I'm some fuckin' girlie you can beat on?"

Eddie Holleran shoved Samantha Lucas off the training table; she fell to the floor hard against the concrete wall. He pulled out a blue-black silenced pistol the same color as

Samantha's wrist from beneath his jacket and shot Esmeralda Ortiz in the head, on the floor, once. The ejected brass shell bounced around between them all like a rubber bouncy ball, the sound of the bullet in the concrete beneath the punctured body sounded like a knock at the door. The smell of powder mixed with the sweet smell of the dead woman's body relaxing its muscles and the instantly growing dark pool of blood. Splattered brain and blood had sprayed everywhere.

Bobby McGarry stooped, collected the empty shell, held it in his hand, stared at Samantha Lucas, said, "Get that wrist looked at, your big fight is tomorrow night. We have a lot of money in on you. Don't let us down or I'll - well, just don't let us down."

She suddenly felt out of control of her life, her destiny, loveless and futureless.

Bobby McGarry dropped a paper bag on the floor as they left the small dressing room, Eddie Holleran was retuning the pistol to the holster under his arm, said, "It has a nice weight, well balanced, and not much kick. You want tacos?"

Eddie Holleran handed his partner the brass shell casing, replied, "Yeah, I could go for tacos."

The door shut and caught the bag, spilling a fan of cash out onto the dull, cold, concrete floor. Samantha Lucas, splattered with blood and bits of skull and brain, gasped, choked, and crawled over to her girlfriend's still and lifeless body. She rubbed Esmeralda Ortiz's thick black bloody hair. She stood, wet a white cotton towel, and wiped the blood from her own face as she spied deeply into an old, bubbled, and cracked mirror. She studied herself, studied her face hard, looking for a self she recognized. She found none. Samantha Lucas turned back to the body on the floor and wiped the blood from Esmeralda Ortiz's ashen face, unable to recognize the living woman she knew in the dead girl's face.

The women lay in bed smoking, Samantha Lucas had told Esmeralda Ortiz, "My Old Man was the worst. When he found out I was a dyke he was all, "Get the fuck out of my house!" And tried to drag me out the front door by my hair. He didn't know I'd been skipping school for years by then and kinda living at the gym. I laid his drunk, fat ass out. When he came to, I was like long gone. That was when I went to Baja. I talked to my little sister. When he recovered himself off the floor from my beating, he went after my ma and sis, hard. That's why I came back and killed him."

She exhaled noisily. They lay in the dark. In the smoke hanging over the small rumpled bed, she illustrated her words with her hands, "I waited outside the house. I smoked and waited in the dark on the road. There were no cars that night. The fat man left our house approached our car parked on the road. I'm good at waiting. Like, I can feel every strand of every muscle in my body and take inventory of all the ways I know how to move faster than everyone else. I snuck out of the shadows, staying quiet, walking on the outsides of my feet. He came out, drunk or hung over or whatever old alcoholics are, and I just walked up to him. I don't know if he knew who I was. I had a hood on. He started to say something. I punched him. Without restraint. Right in his fat face. Only time I ever threw a punch as hard as I could."

Samantha Lucas smoked deeply, confessed, "The fat man fell, bled." She exhaled again, "I felt his nose, his skull crumple in the contact. He dropped hard; blood flowed out of him like wine from a tipped glass. I took his wallet and watch just to make it look like a mugging. That fucker had a few hundred dollars on him. He was always gas lighting my ma into thinking he was broke. I left the cash in the mailbox."

She paused, swallowed, "And I don't regret it. Not any of it. All he ever did was hit me and try to see me naked in the shower."

She lit another cigarette, "I'd stand in the shower and watch through a curtain crack when the fat man pissed and looked for a glimpse of me. I fixed the locks on our doors to keep him out, drunk or sober, at night. We'd each lie in bed and watch the crack beneath our doors, waiting for the shadowed feet to approach, try the doorknob, and leave in frustration. He never said anything but we all knew the score. I would've done anything to spare her what he tried to inflict on me at her age."

They smoked more cigarettes. Esmeralda Ortiz whispered, "Thanks for helping me get out, I knew it would be hard, but I didn't think my Mama would freak out like that. Santa Cachuchas!"

They had moved Esmeralda Ortiz's belongings out from her parent's home earlier that day. The Latino family had come swarming out of a little house on the Los Angeles suburban hillside in the hot bright sun, chasing the girls as they pushed Esmeralda Ortiz's crappy little car down the hill, jumped in after it, slammed the doors, popped the clutch, and sped off. Old women had fallen to their knees praying to Jesus, grown men had watched in disbelief, little kids gave chase, running after them as they sped away and down the hill bouncing over bumps in the asphalt caused by aggressive Eucalyptus tree roots just below the surface.

They kissed in the shadowy darkness, Samantha Lucas told her, "Only time I ever felt good was in Baja. Free of them having left them, but before I came back and killed him. And I feel good in the ring. I feel like one of those crazy tree monkeys in the ring; I can see everything before it happens. Like I know exactly what to counter even before my opponent knows what she's gonna throw."

She gently combed Esmeralda Ortiz's hair with her fingers on the pillow, "You know my ma's new boyfriend is an even bigger piece of shit than my Pop was? Fucking incredible. We should drive down to Baja Sunday morning, just you and me."

Esmeralda Ortiz protested, "Ain't no Puerto Ricans going to Mexico, even if it is just the Baja. That's like the Queen of England going to the Taco Bells or some shit."

They laughed and Samantha Lucas said, "Snobby bitch! You're all a bunch of unwelcome taco-eating Latin parasites to us!"

They laughed more, wrestled, and kissed. Esmeralda Ortiz said, "I still feel funny about the dive. What if it don't look real?"

Samantha Lucas told her, "As long as there's contact it'll look real. No one'll care anyway. They all expect it these days."

"I dunno," Esmeralda Ortiz said, "It still seems weird. It still seems dangerous."

There she was, in a pool of blood, dead even though she never took the dive. Samantha sat and had no idea what to do.

"I can't hide the body, I have no idea how to hide a body," she thought to herself.

She found the ring of keys on the floor beneath Esmeralda Ortiz's lifeless leg, removed the lone car key, dropped the ring back on the floor, stood, picked up her gym bag, it hurt her bruised wrist, and whispered, "Fuck."

She winced in pain all over again.

Samantha Lucas, tears silently falling, walked quickly in the dark of a downtown Los Angeles night. The dirty city seemed even dirtier to her heightened post-fight senses. She approached

Esmeralda Ortiz's small old crappy car, a rusty brown nineteen-seventies Honda Civic parked at a curbside spot without a parking meter on a small one way street, almost an alley, just one block away from the dark stone building that hulked over the boxing arena.

Her hands shook so hard she could barely get the key in the door lock. Eventually she did, opened the squeaky door, hopped in, shut and locked the door, and sighed in relief, then cried loudly. She sat in the dark, steaming up the windows, nearly hyperventilating, crying more out of pain and confusion and fear for her own wellbeing, her own career slipping away from her, than the beautiful boxer she had seduced and lost. Esmeralda Ortiz had been a conquest, a great lay, but Samantha Lucas only really cared about herself. About her plans for getting ahead. Years of training had taught her that.

There was a jarring tap-tap-tap at the window, a Los Angeles police officer dressed in blue stood at the door and shined a light on her face. Samantha Lucas cranked the window down, Officer Tesco asked, "Everything alright?"

Samantha wiped at her face, "Yeah. Everything's fine. I just - lost - broke up with - my fiancé."

She cried some more. The Uniformed officer put the light away, sighed, extracted a pack of cigarettes from her shirt pocket, tapped two out, offered one to Samantha, "That's tough. Here."

Samantha Lucas took the proffered cigarette; the officer lit her own with a match, then lit Samantha. They both exhaled. Her squad car parked at the corner. Its radio squawked.

Officer Tesco pushed her hat back, relaxed, said, "I've been married and divorced two times myself. I love being in love.

"Yeah?" Samantha Lucas looked at the buff blond female police officer, thought, "Maybe I could be a cop?"

Then she agreed, "Me too. A lot"

"You'll be okay," Officer Tesco told her in the voice of a woman who has survived bad and expected still worse, "I know it doesn't help and doesn't seem like it, but you will. Be okay."

Samantha Lucas was unconvinced, wondered, "What would it be like to kiss a woman wearing Kevlar? Body armor was sexy, but this was probably the only non-dyke female cop in all of Los Angeles County."

"I dunno," she said, "I feel pretty crappy."

Officer Tesco agreed, "Yeah. I don't know if you ever stop feeling crappy, but you will be okay."

She smiled and looked as if she wanted to say more, but did not. The squad car radio squawked. Officer Tesco recognized her call number, "I gotta go. You alright?"

Samantha Lucas said, "Yeah, I'm okay."

Walking to the squad car Officer Tesco told her, "There's good tacos two blocks down at the curbside place, maybe you should try getting something eat. I don't want you sitting down here in your car in the dark alone. Go home now."

Samantha Lucas smiled at the novelty of another person's concern for her well-being, even if it was institutional concern, and said, "Thanks, I will."

Officer Tesco got in the squad car, threw it in gear, and sped away, red lights starting to spin. Samantha Lucas sat in the motionless little car, silently smoked, and quietly cried.

Four

Parked at the curb on Zonal Avenue, Samantha Lucas smoked leaning against the small car, absorbing the night, watching the ebb and flow of injured and ambulances around the dilapidated old entrance of the world's busiest trauma center: the emergency room at Los Angeles County Hospital. The mammoth old building looked surreal to her, like a haunted white art deco castle of torture. The stories of malpractice, of incompetence, filled the building so full of ill-served angry souls that their decades of paranormal anger at their wrongful death at the hands of experimental and neglectful surgeons and demented psychiatrists could shake the building to its core or cause it to implode, leaving the true location of a plane of hell in its place.

She dropped her cigarette in the gutter, stuffed her hands into her tracksuit jacket pockets taking care to position her blackened wrist gingerly, and approached the swarming emergency room entrance, avoiding the gang-bangers who smoked and waited for word of their fallen compatriot's status inside, prepared for a long wait and unavoidable, unpredictable humiliation at the hands of at least one over-worked under-paid city employee inside.

The melee was in full Friday night swing. Samantha Lucas sat in her civilian girl jock clothes and waited patiently as the sick, gunshot, stabbed, and crazy of Los Angeles' immigrant, low-income, and under-served communities streamed in and died a little as they waited to be seen. Her mother and father had both been born in this hospital when it was newer, cleaner, and still full of medical promise. When every doctor and nurse had been to war and smoked, and they used whisky to help the sick, and the nurses wore funny starched hats and white dresses with garters and white stockings. As the large hairy man to the left of her vomited blood in a kidney-shaped pink dish and the woman to the right of her smacked her small children, again, a nurse opened a bulletproof door and, reading from a chart in a surly voice, called Samantha Lucas by name.

"Samantha Lucas," Nurse Wilson repeated the name as though she hoped the patient would be found dead in her chair rather than take any of her time, "Samantha Lucas. Samantha Lucas. Samantha Lucas."

Samantha Lucas stood, approached, "I'm Samantha Lucas."

"Samantha Lucas?" Nurse Wilson asked in confirmation.

"Yes, I'm Samantha Lucas." Samantha affirmed, again.

"Follow me, Samantha Lucas," Nurse Wilson turned and led her through the bulletproof enclave down a florescent corridor smelling of bleach, to a medical admissions area no calmer or less crowded than the external waiting area. Standing with her in the hall, Nurse Wilson put an electronic thermometer in a plastic sheath and popped it in Samantha Lucas' mouth, wrapped a blood pressure cuff around her arm, over her tracksuit sleeve, and had her stand on a scale built into the floor and wall more to keep it from being stolen than to alleviate hallway congestion. With the thermometer in her mouth, Nurse Wilson asked a battery of family and pre-existing-condition questions to which Samantha Lucas always answered no. Even if an honest answer had been yes, she lived in strict denial that she ever had a family, thinking of her parents more as evil adoptive guardians so she could maintain the myth of family in her mind, and keep it alive as a future possibility for her life on her own.

Reading from the chart Nurse Wilson asked, "It says here you think you sprained your left hand. What were you doing at the time to hurt it?"

Samantha Lucas told her, "I'm a fighter. I had a fight tonight and hit my opponent on her skull. I heard something pop. I felt something pop, in my hand. I think I dislocated a bone or sprained something."

The nurse disconnected her from the cuff and the thermometer and guided her to sit on a gurney in the busy hallway, and rolled up the left track sleeve. Samantha had wrapped a red and black Lonsdale hand wrap used for training hastily around her wrist. She now unwound the long length of fabric, slowly, exposing the wrist for the nurse to look at, feel, and inspect.

"Mmmhmm," Nurse Wilson asked, "What? You're a boxer?"

Samantha Lucas smiled, proud as always, "Yeah. A prizefighter. I'm undefeated."

Nurse Wilson was not impressed; she scribbled a note, "Wow. That is very impressive. Keep this chart, a doctor will see you shortly."

And walked away.

Samantha Lucas sat, chart on her lap, back to the wall, and fell promptly asleep. In what felt like a minute but was obviously many hours judging by the change of patients in the area, two doctors were gently waking her from her random, absorbing dreams. Samantha Lucas jumped at their touch, saw where she was, remembered her wrist, focused on the doctor reading her chart, and cradled her arm as they read.

the younger doctor, Doctor Edwin James, said, "Good morning, Missus Lucas my name is Doctor James, this is Doctor Roberts, we're here to take a look at your - left - hand?"

They saw her black hand, each stared hard, Doctor Cindy Roberts said, "Wow, look at that. May I?"

She was tall and slim and had long brown hair and a gentle touch although her fingers were cold. She took Samantha Lucas gently by the hand, felt her wrist, gingerly tugged her fingers, thumb, pressed different places around the immobile left hand. Samantha Lucas flinched but said nothing.

Doctor Cindy Roberts said, "Seriously fractured. In more than one place. How did you do this again?"

She gingerly handed the black wrist to her colleague who palpated it a little less gently although with warmer hands.

Samantha Lucas flinched a little more, said, "I'm a boxer. An underground boxer. The champion of my weight class."

They looked at her in wonder, Doctor Roberts made a note in the chart, Doctor James asked, "Underground boxer?"

Samantha Lucas told them, "I fight in illegal prize fights downtown. In small arenas beneath the tall buildings. For the mob."

Both Doctor James and Doctor Roberts were visibly impressed, Doctor Roberts said, "I had no idea. There are illegal mob boxing matches? With girl fighters?"

Samantha Lucas smiled; she had a crooked toothy smile, "Yeah. You'd be surprised I'm undefeated. I'm eleven and oh with no ties and seven KO's."

She breathed deeply, the impact of her new record hitting her suddenly; she wiped back a tear and took another deep breath.

Doctor James asked, looking over the chart, "How old are you? Twenty?"

Samantha Lucas agreed, "I'll be twenty next week. I have a really big fight late tonight. I need you guys to fix my wrist so I can go get some rest."

The doctors looked at each other, the doctor-look they can't help but give each other that tells the observant patient exactly what they are thinking, and that it's not good. Samantha Lucas missed the look.

Doctor Roberts said, "Your hand is broken. We're sending you upstairs for an x-ray. You need to plan on wearing a cast for the next three months, at least."

Samantha Lucas was taken aback, visibly, instantly shaken, "I what? It what? I can't. It can't be broken. I have a fight tonight. I might have fights scheduled for next month. I can't miss them. I --"

Doctor James interrupted, "You're done fighting. At least for a while. Maybe forever. Your wrist is broken. Fractured."

Samantha Lucas felt like he had punched her in the chest, "But. I'm going pro. Going legit. What am I gonna do? These guys'll - if I don't fight I - I can't not fight I can't wear a cast. I --

Doctor James told her, "You need to make other plans. You need to take care of your hand."

Doctor Roberts suggested, "We can write a note for you explaining what happened. We can --"

Samantha Lucas interrupted her, "A note? These guys don't read notes. I can't take them a Doctor's note. Jesus Christ. This is all I know how to do. This is all I'm good at."

Doctor James failed to try to console her, "You'll need to sit out for the next few months. Most likely, it won't knit well enough to ever box again. You need to consider this."

Samantha Lucas was baffled, "But, then, who will I be? You don't understand: this is who I am."

They had no reply for her.

"And the fans love me. They love me for it. Without it, I'll be nobody. When I'm boxing, I'm somebody. Without it, I'll be a bum."

Neither doctor said a word. Samantha Lucas looked even tougher with her heart breaking.

, Doctor Roberts offered, "Let's get an x-ray so we know exactly what we're talking about before we start making any other plans. Okay?"

Samantha Lucas sighed, cradled, and looked at her bruised and swollen hand, "This is all I'm good at."

Doctor James told her gently, "Just one x-ray."

Nearly twelve hours later Samantha Lucas emerged from the bottomless pit of county health care into the warmth of the noonday sun. They x-rayed her wrist and arm, against her better-judgment they applied a fiberglass cast over what they found, and they gave her a scribbled-on piece of paper and a voucher for pain pills they said would make her constipated. She walked to Esmeralda Ortiz's car, dropping all the paper work, the prescription, and the voucher in a curbside trash can.

She plucked the parking tickets off the windshield, the singular advantage of a dead girlfriend being unfettered parking of the dead girlfriend's car until it got booted or towed. She hopped in and drove back downtown to the taco stand near the arena. She parked in front of the little eatery at a red curb, walked past the plate glass windows to the door, entered, and seated herself in a vinyl booth. Her favorite waitress, Martina, came over with a plastic cup of ice and a big plastic pitcher full of sweet cold rice milk.

"Hey Sammy, how you today sweetie?" Martina poured the horchata and chewed her gum.

Samantha said, "Tired Martina. I'm tired. Can I get my usual but can I also get a nice big steak, cooked medium with onions and peppers, please?"

Martina smiled wide, raised her eyebrows, "Wish I could eat like you, but then I'd have to train like you. My ass is too square already. Be right back with your tacos."

Martina returned to the lunch counter and attended to her other customers, told the Latino short order cook behind the stainless steel serving shelf Samantha Lucas' order. In a moment, a plate of tacos and whole beans and rice and a plate covered with a big thin, flat, crispy steak, ashy gray, sat in front of her with bottles of hot sauce and jars of spicy relishes. Another paper plate covered with tacos wrapped in clear plastic wrapped waited on the table for later. Samantha sat and ate, so hungry after the trouble of the previous night and the day spent at the hospital. When she finished the meal, she flipped some bills onto the table and put the thin steak knife with the wooden riveted handle into her tracksuit jacket pocket.

Samantha Lucas returned the car to a curbside space in the alley with no parking meters, near the arena and snuck back inside, mixing in with the insurance and finance workers from the many floors above. In her dressing room, she sat with her cast resting on a small table next to a hot plate. The paper plate of tacos at her elbow. She smoked and sawed at the fiberglass cast slowly, deliberately, with the stolen steak knife. Eventually she was able to peel it off with her teeth. She removed the thin gauze dressings and looked at her blue wrist, began gently taping it in white zinc oxide tape using her other good hand and her teeth. After she covered the bruising, she taped the other wrist to match and then ate a few pain pills out of a prescription bottle a trainer gave her a few years earlier. Real painkillers with fewer side effects than the watery ones the doctor at county had prescribed for her. Her mind would stay sharp and feel no pain from the small fractured bones. She washed the pills down with two eggs she cracked into a jelly glass, old school style. Then took a big bite of taco stood to study her reflection in the full-length shiny sheet of steel bolted to the wall that served as a mirror while working the speed bag at the other end of her small dressing room, with just her right.

Hours later the roar of the crowd deafened Samantha Lucas, as she stood behind the curtain, ready to fight again. Her taped wrists, she told herself, should attract no attention. She stood still; eyes squeezed shut, her mind rushing on the roar of the fans. She heard her name and pulled the curtain away, danced out into the intimate old arena, looking mean and enthusiastic. She shadowboxed her way to the ring as the Irish punk rock blared and the fans hollered. She took the stairs, maneuvered the ropes, and spared around the ring.

Mills Neumann announced the challenger and hyperactive, World Beat, African music boomed from the ringside P.A. The alternate curtain opened and a sinewy, coal-black woman stood with black-taped balled-fists on her hips, her hair corn-rowed back and down her head, wearing all black silks, black boots with black laces, and a red mouth guard making her look beautiful and sinister-looking at once. She broke her pose, pranced down the aisle toward the ring, stopping every few feet to mock brawl, and easily knocks her imaginary opponent down. She would then kiss her fists in turn and hold them over her head in victory while smiling the red, sinister, apple-cheeked smile around to the crowd. They loved it.

Samantha Lucas had heard of the South African woman, Nonni Bindonna, but had never met her and never fought her before that night. Nonni Bindonna strode down the aisle, hopped up the stairs, and leaped over the ropes into the ring in one bound. The crowd roared. She scissored her arms over her head, and walked the ring as though Samantha were not sharing it with her, leading the crowd chanting, "Nonni-boom-ah-yay! Nonni-boom-ah-yay!"

Literally "Nonni kill her," just as the African fans had yelled to Muhammad Ali when he fought George Foreman in Zaire in nineteen seventy-four. It unnerved Samantha Lucas, and soon the entire arena chanted, "Nonni-boom-ah-yay! Nonni-boom-ah-yay!" They followed the lead of the beautiful African woman with the red mouth who waved her arms slowly in rhythm to the chanting like a young bird slowly flapping its long wings. Samantha Lucas already felt like she had lost. The bell ding-ding-dinged and the chanting died slowly down.

Mills Neumann announced each fighter, but Samantha Lucas still had the sting of the crowd's chant in her ears and she heard nothing else. She felt angry and crazy, she felt betrayed and alone. The preliminaries complete, the bald referee brought the two sweaty, muscular women to the center of the ring, inspected and held their taped fists, said again, as always, the arena's unofficial mantra, "You both know the rules; I don't need a clean fight: just a good fight. Bump fists and come out swinging."

Nonni Bindonna smiled a sarcastic grin at Samantha Lucas and there was an eye drawn on the red mouth guard in black. A football-shaped oval with a circle in the center with a single dot in the circle of that. Samantha Lucas stared at the eye in the woman's mouth and the Nonni Bindonna laughed a funny, muffled chuckle with her teeth in the thick mouth guard.

They bumped fists, receded, the bell dinged, and they came out swinging. Samantha knew with the first punch thrown she was better than the challenger was. The other woman's timing was off, she lead with the hand she planned to use next, she kept her hands balled into tight fists, wasting her energy. At a young age, trainers taught Samantha Lucas to keep her hands loose until the second of impact, conserving her energy. The challenger was scared. Putting on a show to hide her fear.

"Fear of what?" Samantha Lucas wondered, easily blocking and deflecting every punch thrown, feeling like a grown up pillow fighting an enthusiastic three year old.

She did not need her left. Samantha Lucas just kept it up and circled right to keep it out of harm's way and to keep the challenger, who wanted to circle the other direction, off balance. Samantha Lucas wanted to knock the woman's mouth guard down into her throat with a single punch, but she waited. Soon the bell dinged and both receded back to the plastic-tasting lukewarm water waiting in their opposite corners while the ring model held the placard high over her head and made her circuit.

Another ding and Samantha Lucas decided to pummel the African fighter with her right as much as she could while keeping the ringside scoring even and avoiding knocking her out. Soon the other woman had blood from open cuts above her eyebrows streaming down the sides of her head and in her hair. Her nose was wet with blood and snot, and fat swollen bruised lips, cracked and bleeding, obscured the drawing etched into the plastic mouth guard. Samantha Lucas had hardly broken a sweat. Again, the bell rang. Again, they retreated and drank the waiting water. A medic applied styptic powder and sticky butterfly sutures to Nonni Bindonna's cuts. The ring model walked the circle of the ring, placard over her head, while attempting to avoid inserting her lethal red stilettos into the smeared and splattered thick dark blood on the canvas.

Sixty seconds later they were circling the ring again, Samantha Lucas toying with the challenger until the African landed a right jab to Samantha Lucas' chin that laid her out. She fell hard, and remained, unaware and out-cold past the eight seconds required for the other woman to win the match. As Mills Neumann helped the dejected champion to her feet amidst the deafening roar of the elated and irate crowd, she stole a glance at the woman who had bested her, who returned her look and spit blood and a long, yellow, broken tooth onto the sweat-and-blood-damp canvas.

Samantha smiled for an instant and then hid her face in a white cotton ringside towel. At the referee's count the crowd had begun to surge on the ring, once Samantha was on her feet someone threw an old wooden official's chair into the ring and fans began swarming over the sides and over the ropes attacking Mills Neumann, Nonni Bindonna, and Samantha Lucas, each of whom took measures to defend themselves until the security men employed by Eddie Holleran and Bobby McGarry, Irish hooligans with shaved heads and shamrocks tattooed to their pale freckled skulls wearing dark suit jackets over football jerseys, streamed through the crowd with cricket bats and up onto the elevated ringside and began pummeling any fan foolish enough to have entered the ring or to approach the bracing cables. As the melee ensued, the promoters escorted the fighters and the referee to a hastily unlocked and opened nearby trapdoor at the foot of the ring where the three disappeared down a rusty ladder into dark, damp, and steamy concrete-boiler-room-hissing silence.

In the dark Mills Neumann grabbed Samantha Lucas by the meat of her biceps and squeezed hard, spitting, "What the fuck was that? Goddamn. I just lost fifteen hundred bucks on you! Fuck!"

He stormed away, up the concrete corridor lighting a cigarette and muttering. Samantha Lucas turned to walk to her dressing room and found Nonni Bindonna in her way, filling the narrow corridor. The woman looked like a side of beef.

In accented English and the lisp of a bruised mouth with broken teeth she said, "You humiliate me."

Samantha Lucas punched the woman in the face with her right, with restraint, dropping the new champ to the dirty concrete floor where she remained without moving as Samantha Lucas said, "Boom-ah-yay, bitch," and walked away.

She navigated the dark tunnels until she came to familiar territories that lead to her small dressing room. Exhausted and disgusted with herself, Samantha Lucas sat on the old padded training table and stared at the ground at the dark stain on the concrete below her dangling feet. At a single hard knock on her door she flinched, Eddie Holleran and Bobby McGarry entered the still little room. They said nothing. For a minute that seemed like an hour all three stared at the ground. A tear rolled down Samantha Lucas's cheek, she waited for the shot.

Eddie Holleran said, "Ah Jesus Christ. What the fuck were you thinking?"

Samantha Lucas stammered, whispered, "I -- I dunno."

Bobby McGarry asked, "Did you have to fucking humiliate her? Break her fucking tooth out? One handed? Did you think no one else would notice that up there?"

Eddie Holleran said, "Get the fuck out of here. I don't ever want to see you or hear from you again." He handed her another brown paper bag stuffed with cash, "Here."

Bobby McGarry grinned a little, "Even though you fucked up the dive we still made more off this fight than all your other fights combined."

Eddie Holleran put his arm around her, she stiffened, braced herself for pain, instead he said, "Let this be a lesson to you: it's always more profitable to be paid to not do what you're good at, than it is to be paid to do what you're good at. That's why rackets work."

Samantha Lucas sighed as the big man chucked her gently on her chin, said, "I get that now. I'm finished guys. The doctors said my wrist is broken if four places and'll be glass for the rest of my life. Only chance I have is to train to be right handed."

Bobby McGarry joked, "Or marry one of the fucking doctors."

Eddie Holleran muttered, "Fucking Doctors."

Bobby McGarry asked, "Did they take an x-ray.

Samantha Lucas said, "Yeah. They showed me the fractures."

Eddie Holleran muttered, "Fucking x-rays."

Samantha Lucas confessed, "Guys, I've got nothing now. Am nothing now."

The two big men looked at each other, a little sad, a little confused by their role in consoling her. If she had not had Irish parents, they knew they would have just killed her and kept her money. People in common meant a lot to the two men, so they wanted to do right by her. If she could mend her left and build up her right, they could still get a slice of her legitimate career, however long or short it eventually played out to be.

Eddie Holleran told her, "No. You're fast. You're strong. You're smart, and good-looking; you've got your whole life ahead of you."

Bobby McGarry agreed, "You're young. Young counts for a lot. Young counts for everything."

Five

At the world's busiest trauma center on a warm summer Saturday night, Samantha Lucas stood at the reception desk of the emergency room attempting to explain her situation, again, clearly to the admitting nurse, who, overworked, underpaid, and unappreciated, was late for her break.

"No, I was here yesterday." Samantha Lucas tried to maintain her calm, tried to remain polite, "And they put a cast on my broken wrist. I needed to cut it off. So I cut it off. So now I need a new cast."

Nurse Nguyen glared at her. The absurdity of patient's without insurance, whom, it turned out, did not want to get better, burned at, and humiliated the core of her personality, of why she became a nurse, of why she thought she wanted to spend her life helping people.

"God knows it was not for the glamour, of which there is none or the gratitude, of which there is even less," she thought, as the jock woman talked at her.

She recognized crazy when it came in the door and paraded as sane, "You were here in this emergency room yesterday? They saw you, admitted you, x-rayed you, orthopedics put a cast on your arm, and then you left, cut the cast off, and have come back today for - another cast?"

She paused and glared at the crazy bitch in the tired tracksuit, then smiled, saccharin sweet, her teeth freshly whitened and almost transparent, "We do not put new casts on every day. If your wrist is broken, you need to leave the cast on. Otherwise it won't heal."

Samantha Lucas sighed, "I know that. I needed my wrist out of the cast for a fight last night. Now I need the cast so my wrist heals."

Nurse Nguyen raised her eyebrows, "How do we know you won't just take it off again? How did you get it off?"

Samantha Lucas confessed, "I cut it off with a knife. A steak knife."

Nurse Nguyen asked, "You cut your cast off your wrist with a steak knife? Do you have the steak knife, or any knives, or any other weapons, with you now?"

Samantha Lucas was confused, "No. No. Of course not. What? You're not listening to me, I need a new cast."

Nurse Nguyen stared through Samantha Lucas, said, "I am listening to you. Have a seat and someone will be with you shortly."

Exasperated, Samantha Lucas returned to the waiting area where there were no empty chairs. The large motion-activated double sliding glass doors beyond the guards and metal detectors opened and closed so often they beat out an awkward rhythm for the hustle and bustle, like the backstage of theatre on opening night. She stood, back to a wall, exhausted. For the first time in a long time, but as she had now for the entire day, Samantha Lucas felt lost and confused.

She wondered, "Without boxing and obsessive training, what will I pin my sanity to? Just training little kids?"

She closed her eyes. When she opened them again, the faces had all changed, the sun was on the rise, and clouds littered the sky. Across the street, the buildings glowed orange in the dawn.

A prim, diminutive man in khakis and a sweater-vest, social worker Robert Stevenson, holding a chart, called out Samantha Lucas' name through the opening in the bulletproof enclosure, "Samantha Lucas?"

Samantha Lucas shook herself awake, looked at the guards in rented uniforms next to the metal detectors at the entrance, tried to recall where she was, realized she was back at the hospital, and croaked, "Here. Me. I'm here."

She grabbed her duffle bag, approached the thick sheets of poly carbonate-clad glass, and passed into the admissions area.

Robert Stevenson said, "Hi Samantha, I'm Robert, follow me?"

They threaded down the hallway past more bulletproof glass enclosures, past gurneys of sick and dying patients, past open doors of squabbling families, one family member inevitably in bed, silent, staring up at the television on the wall or out the door into the hallway beyond. Past nurses trailing white coat doctors or retrieving blue scrub orderlies with mops and stacks clean linens. They entered a lonely, stark, and sterile office with an empty metal desk, empty metal trash can, and two cushioned metal chairs, one on either side of the empty desk. Each of them took a seat, Robert Stevenson behind the desk.

He opened her chart, reviewed the admitting nurse's notes for a moment, looked up at Samantha Lucas, steepled his fingertips, and asked, "Okay, and why are you here today?

She told him, "I need a new cast for my broken wrist."

Robert Stevenson said, "Mmmhmm, and you were here before, when?"

Samantha Lucas confessed, "Yesterday."

He did not look up from her chart, asked, "Did you see a doctor when you were here yesterday?"

Samantha Lucas sighed, "Yes. I saw two Doctors. They looked at my wrist, sent me upstairs for an x-ray, and had someone set my wrist in a cast."

Robert Stevenson looked up at her, studied her arms, "Which wrist?"

Samantha Lucas held up the bruised wrist in question, remaining calm, "This one, my left."

Robert Stevenson looked at her, asked slowly, "Okay, so, do you think your wrist is in a cast now?"

Samantha Lucas was truly puzzled, "No. No? No. Of course not. I cut it off."

Robert Stevenson scribbled a long note in her chart with his pen and asked without looking up, "Why?"

Samantha Lucas looked up at the yellowed fiberglass ceiling squares, asked, "Honestly?

Robert Stevenson stopped writing, looked up from the chart at her, "Yes Samantha. Honestly."

Samantha Lucas recited the answer she knew so well, the answer that she knew would clear nothing up, "I had to throw a fight or the promoters would have killed me like they killed my girlfriend."

Robert Stevenson looked at her, did not say anything, and then scribbled more notes.

Eventually he asked, "How did you cut the cast off?

Samantha Lucas was done, "What?

He repeated the question, "How did you cut the cast off?"

She told him, "With a knife, with a steak knife."

Then he asked her slowly, "Do you still have the knife, do you have it with you now?"

Samantha Lucas said, "No of course not. It's in my locker. Are you a Doctor?"

He told her, "I'm a graduate student. Do you live in a house or an apartment?"

Samantha Lucas said, "Neither, I live at the arena, in my locker room."

He asked, "Do you live alone?"

Samantha Lucas said, "I do now. You're not a doctor? When do I get to see the doctor? I need to know when I can fight again.

Robert Stevenson raised his eyebrows, scribbled, and asked slowly, "Why would you need to fight?"

Calmly at first, then with growing malice, Samantha Lucas told him, "I am a fucking boxer. I just told you that. I broke my wrist fighting my girlfriend. I fight for the fucking Irish mafia and they had me throw my fight last night. I could not fight with a fucking cast on my fucking wrist so I took it off. I stole a steak knife from Taco Time and sawed it off. They killed my fucking girlfriend the night before last. I thought they were going to kill me. Now I am done. I need to get my wrist set again and if you are not a fucking doctor who can do that then I just waited around here all night for no fucking reason."

Scribbling, looking up at her then back at her chart, "Are you left or right handed?"

Samantha Lucas punched a hole in the wall over his desk, gypsum dust settled on her chart under his hands, she smiled at him, "Right."

The social worker jumped from his seat, rushed past her, and punched a big red button on the wall next to the door as he fled into the hall calling for help. Two huge orderlies and a rent-a-cop ran in, tackled Samantha Lucas off the chair onto the cold hard floor and pinned her by her broken wrist.

She screamed, pain ran through her from her left arm, and she landed a right into the throat of one orderly on his knees trying to get a firm hold of her right arm, sending him sprawling against the wall where he started choking and coughing blood as the rent-a-cop pinned her by her face to the ground with his bent knee and shin across the back of her neck, keeping her face to the ground. She felt like her face would explode and she felt her head turning purple. All was chaos as the other orderly screamed for help, the rent-a-cop tried to call for backup on his Walkie Talkie, and the injured orderly began to turn purple from a lack of breath. The social worker stood watching, crying, warm urine soaking down his trouser legs and into his shoes and socks.

Samantha Lucas swore at them all promising death and destruction on all their heads between gasps for breath. As she screamed, emergency room physicians swarmed in, lay the suffocating orderly on his back, and worked to clear his airway free of broken larynx. More uniformed officers gathered and held her down, taking extra care to wrench her arms and to hurt her as much as possible until an intern on a psych-rotation appeared in white coat, brandishing a hypodermic swiftly injected into Samantha Lucas' taught writhing right butt-cheek, sedating her almost instantly.

As her eyes and mind drooped she noticed the curtain of onlookers watching from the doorway make room for the orderly, now on a gurney, to be relocated to a trauma room. The social worker standing nearby in tears, dark stains down his pants Doctor Cindy Roberts looking in, eating a sandwich, and drinking coffee from a paper cup with a lid.

Cindy Roberts studied Samantha Lucas as she was being restrained, stepped on, wrists bent, injected, and she noticed the hole in the wall. She noted the startled, weeping, social worker who had pissed himself.

She stepped forward, and asked between bites, "What are you doing to my patient?"

The guards all looked up at her. A velvet purple curtain fell over the small hospital office in Samantha Lucas' head, leaving her alone, lying in the center of a sedate boxing ring, on an island of calm, floating upon distant sun-dappled morning clouds.

Samantha Lucas slept in a hard skinny bed in a ward full of hard skinny beds full of crazy people. Doctor Cindy Roberts stood at the foot of her bed looking at her chart. Slowly Samantha Lucas stirred, blinked, looked around, picked up her wrist, it was in a new cast and cuffed, as was her right, to the bedsides in leather and Velcro restraints. For a moment, Doctor Cindy Roberts was Esmeralda Ortiz and Samantha Lucas was relieved.

Cindy Roberts' voice broke her relief, "I wrote my name and service number on this one, but if you cut your cast off again you might want to consider making an appointment at my office for the next one."

Samantha Lucas smiled, groggy, asked, "What happened?"

Doctor Cindy Roberts looked at her, studying the restrained woman's face for indications of disguised malice, "You scared our social worker when you punched that hole in his office wall. They sedated you. It took three big guys to restrain you. They messed your wrist up even more. You nearly killed one of them, Roberto Martinez. You broke his larynx and he nearly suffocated since you collapsed his airway. You're pretty strong, and lucky he's alive. You scared the shit out of everyone. I have you here in the psych-ward on a seventy-two hour psych-hold. You were in the jail-ward for two days; it took me that long to get you transferred here. I think they wanted to keep you knocked-out, so they had you on a drip. You've been drugged asleep, sedated, for nearly three days. Not exactly standard operating care."

Tears welled in Samantha Lucas' eyes. She sniffed hard.

Cindy Roberts continued, "They decided to drop the charges against you because Roberto Martinez torqued your broken wrist. The lawyers want to avoid counter suits. I have paperwork they gave me for you to sign. It basically states you agree to never, ever come back here again unless brought by paramedics because you're dying. They cannot legally ban you because of federal and state funding restrictions, but they want to discourage you from ever coming back. I think they obtained restraining orders for the entire E.R. staff against you too."

Samantha Lucas muttered, "Fuck."

Cindy Roberts continued, "I declined to have one. I vouched for you, said that I didn't think you presented a risk based on our time together during your initial admission and because Robert Stevenson is a patronizing prick at best. If you sign the papers and promise to never come back here, ever, I can have the cuffs removed and the hospital won't press charges."

Samantha Lucas said, "Wow, I promise I can pay for the damage."

Doctor Cindy Roberts raised her hand, "Not necessary, the room needed new paint anyway. I can remove the right restraint, but need a key for the left."

She pressed the nurse's call button and unstrapped one of the complex leather and Velcro clasps, "Here, sign these."

She handed Samantha Lucas the clipboard that had been resting on the foot of her bed.

Taking the clipboard Samantha Lucas asked, "Where, got a pen?"

"Just flip through the pages," Cindy Roberts told her handing her a ballpoint pen, "Legal highlighted all the lines for you to sign. You made a lot of paper work. This should finish it off."

The other young physician from Samantha Lucas's initial admission, Doctor Edwin James, approached Cindy Roberts tentatively at the foot of Samantha Lucas' bed as a nurse came over and dubiously began unlocking the other cuff from Samantha Lucas' cast-covered wrist.

"Hey Cindy, can I get your unofficial opinion on something?" He asked shyly.

Doctor Cindy Roberts watched the nurse unlock the cuff, "Hey Ed. If you need a consultation you should call up for one."

Doctor James whispered, "It's not like that - I just need your opinion."

Doctor Cindy Roberts sighed, smiled tightly, "Okay, give me a minute?"

Doctor James was relieved, "Oh yeah, sure, I'm over here."

He strolled away too look at another patient, Doctor Cindy Roberts' pager beeped, she unhooked it from the tied waist-band of her green scrub pants, and muttered as she read the electronic text, "Always with the curbside-consultation. Jesus Christ."

The nurse left and Samantha Lucas spied her clothes on a nearby chair, her duffle bag resting beneath. She returned the clipboard, papers signed, to the foot of the bed and hopped out, barefoot, onto the cold floor. She spread her legs, reached up her gown, and slowly removed the catheter, wincing slightly. Then pulled the tape off her arm, slowly removed the needles, rested them on the bed, and put the tape back on the bruised punctures in her arm like band-aids, and peeled her cotton medical gown off.

Cindy Roberts looked up from her pager in time to see Samantha Lucas' tattoo in the area of her shaved-smooth pubic bone, just above the V of her crotch, the single word CURBSIDE in the style of the Everlast logo, like a bow tie in a rectangle, the C and the E in CURBSIDE taller than the other letters, inked to look just like a boxer's waistband logo, but far below the belt. Cindy Roberts blushed. The other patients in the ward began to howl, Cindy Roberts quickly wheeled a nearby white cloth and metal screen over and arranged it around Samantha Lucas as she dressed herself.

Cindy Roberts tried to avert her eyes, but Samantha Lucas was so oblivious, so comfortably naked, hairless, tan, absurdly muscled but without the physical oddity and ugliness of a habitual steroid user, and had that wicked tattoo, that Cindy Roberts bit the tip of her ball point pen, hard.

Samantha Lucas got dressed, continually oblivious, stooped, and collected her duffle bag.

Strap over her shoulder, she extended her hand, "Thanks again Doc."

Cindy Roberts took the proffered hand, said, "Don't hesitate to call if you need anything."

Samantha Lucas smiled, asked, "Yeah? You got any money?"

Cindy Roberts was surprised, disappointed, acquiesced, "Sure, yeah, of course," and pulled a crush of random wadded bills from a deep white coat pocket,

Samantha Lucas grinned, "Naw Doc, I was just kidding around. See ya's!"

She walked down the aisle between the feet of the other beds, and through the massive glass and steel double doors, met by a uniformed security guard who escorted her to the elevators and outside to the curb.

Cindy Roberts watched her leave, weighing how sane Samantha Lucas seemed with how crazy she had acted three nights before. She worked to help people for a living; Samantha Lucas punched people and people punched her in turn, for a living. She lived in the confines of problem solving: symptoms, history, physical background versus treatments, drugs, therapies. Samantha Lucas lived in the confines of her body: strength, speed, agility versus her opponent.

She was a little scared of Samantha Lucas, and totally intrigued. Any woman who could nearly kill a massive orderly with one shot, from her weaker arm, was a woman to fear respect not easily forgotten. The pager beeped again, whispering she replied, too late, "See ya's."

Six

Linda O'Brien parked the little English convertible in the labyrinth-like massive subterranean parking garage deep below the surface streets. She lost her way twice looking for the elevators amongst the hundreds of other parked cars and settled for the wide metal stairwell that clanged loudly every time her heels hit another step, sounding like a massive damaged harpsichord capable of one single deep dull note.

Atop the stairs, she crossed the sterile landscaped courtyard and approached the massive glass wall of doors that lead inside to the stealthy and secure entrance of Conway Productions. She pressed the intercom button, waited, smiled into the small camera lens, and a voice asked something indiscernible.

Linda O'Brien replied, "Good morning, Linda O'Brien, I have a ten o'clock with Ted Conway."

The door buzzed and she pulled the massive handle, swinging the frosted glass door out into the hall, making an opening large enough for a refrigerator to be wheeled through. She entered the quiet of the lush office suite and looked down the cubicle row of little old ladies who, hired when they were young by long-forgotten middle-aged managers now retired or dead, worked for different middle-aged men and women down the row of windowed offices.

She was motioned along to the back of the suite, down the long massive corridor littered with decades of photos and show memorabilia, signed photographs of many of the world's famous, now dead, who tuned in long ago. The legacy of a television show that outlived its fans, its cast, and its creators suddenly seemed grotesque, a lifeless electronic entity outliving them all, it seemed cyborg to her.

Ted Conway emerged from his office, his hand extended, and greeted her enthusiastically, "Linda my shining star, how is this glorious day treating you so far?"

She noted his handmade suit, shirt, and shoes. Felt a fleeting pang of Hollywood envy, "Oh Ted, I'm fantastic!"

"Never is heard a discouraging word," the first tenant of Executive Producer meetings, floated to the forefront of her mind as she answered him, shook his hand, and they shared a small quick emotionless embrace.

He was gorgeous and in charge and dapper and she was terrified of him.

"He is larger than life," she thought to herself as he lead her back into his massive palatial office and found all his executive's-in-charge-of-production and attorneys and accountants waiting, as usual, in a half-circle around the back of Ted Conway's favorite chair.

She sat across from them after they exchanged more emotionless pleasantries. She laid a sheaf of papers on the massive table with the in-laid sundial in front of Ted Conway's chair. He eyed it like a banker spying a silver dollar down a curbside gutter.

Seated across the huge coffee table from her Ted Conway reached out and opened the binder, carefully pulling back the big rubber band that held the folder shut, and picked up page after page of script. He read voraciously through black words on white pages and held each he finished over his shoulder for Mark Ellison to take and read, who read and handed each page to Brent, who read and handed each page to Grant, who read and handed each page to Randy, who read and placed each page neatly back on the table in a new pile, face down. Linda O'Brien sat and watched this in wonder, since she had couriered and emailed the pages to the entire production and executive teams nearly every day for over a week. Ted Conway finished. The others continued to read and pass the pages.

Ted Conway sat, stared at her, then grinned, exclaimed, "Holy Fucking Christ wearing a red, white, and green yarmulke on a Cross at Christmas: we're gonna win more Emmys!"

He launched from around the coffee table, past the weird sundial, and pumped Linda O'Brien's hand, "God dammit I'm always right! The longer I live the more I know that! You're right on track. I don't know how you people do it - I can barely right a grocery list! Hell, only thing I can write is checks, but you're hitting all the right arcs, in spades!"

Everyone reading agreed, nodded, Linda O'Brien smiled, Ted Conway let go of her hand and resumed his seat across from her, continued, "Promoting you was genius, shear genius! We're back on the big board, the sponsors are happy, the network is happy, the viewers are fucking ecstatic. Sexy lesbian Irish mafia jocks; who knew they would be the darlings of network fucking daytime T.V?"

No one answered, still he waited patiently, unwilling to continue until Mark Ellison, understanding he missed his cue exclaimed, "You! You Ted! You knew!"

"That's right I did! No wonder I'm in charge. Hey, where are we eating today?"

Mark Ellison, handing all the pages he failed to read to the next reader fished in his pockets until her came up with his Palm Pilot, "Today is Tuesday Ted. Taco Tuesday. We're going to Tres Amigos Muertos for tacos."

Ted Conway clapped his hands, rubbed them together, "Good, good! Call ahead and tell Manuel I don't want anything red on the table or in the food. No red today, we're on a roll and I don't need the color red fucking things up at lunch."

Mark Ellison was concerned, "Uh, but what about the salsa and the red tortilla chips mixed in with the green and yellow ones, Ted?"

Ted Conway thought, then told him, "Send someone ahead, an intern, to take all the red chips out of the bowls and to replace the Salsa Rojo, with Salsa Verde!"

Mark Ellison agreed, "Okay Ted!"

The tall man quickly exited the office to locate an intern as the other staff kept on reading.

Ted Conway looked at Linda O'Brien, stared at her, then said, "I was talking to my pastor the other week, and he told me something that struck me as peculiar, but I now understand. You know what he told me, Linda?"

Linda O'Brien wondered if the pastor told him he was as nutty as elephant shit. She shook her head, afraid of what any pastor might tell this man.

"No?" He asked seeming genuinely surprised, as though she should be able to tell him.

, he said, "He told me he would trade every pious person he ever knew for just one humanitarian."

He let the weight of that sit in the room.

"And I applied it to you, to your promotion. I traded my devotees, the show's tried and true groupies, the faithful, the show's pious production insiders, long-term writing staff, for you: a human writer, an east coast writer, an outside writer, with a different perspective I was right."

He paused, recalled Mark Ellison had left and could not affirmatively punctuate his assertion, so he moved on, satisfied with himself regardless.

He dismissed his staff, "Guys, go wait in the hall, I want some time alone with Linda here."

They filed out of the room and into the hall, a few feet from the massive doors, without so much as a murmur. After the doors shut, he leaned in, gazed at her again, and asked, "Now, tell me. How exactly you know the woman boxer?"

Linda nearly choked, stalled, "Uh, I made her up? I made it all up."

Ted Conway grinned, "Yeah right. I was at the fight where she took that dive against the African fighter. I lost thirty grand on that fight. I was also at the fight where she broke her fucking wrist, but we had no idea she busted it, or that is was broken during the fight the next night. So tell me, how do you know her?"

Linda scrambled, lied, "She's a friend of my hairdresser's? Well a friend of my hairdresser's daughter. They know each other and my hairdresser told me the high points, I filled in the rest, added the dialogue, the relationships, the actions, and reactions."

Her lie seemed to appease Ted Conway.

He smiled slowly, "Well find out when her next fight is and what the fix is, because I want my money back. I hate to tell you, I was pretty pissed to find there was a fix by reading your outlines. It looked so real. I suppose that is what I deserve for gambling on the fights but the horses are no better. I'm not pious, obviously, so I try to be more humanitarian; I give all my winnings to my church. I guess I'm not very good at either."

He stood, walked to the doors, opened them, said, "Let's go everybody, I'm hungry today!"

He turned to Linda, still seated in the massive chair, called to her, "Keep up the good work! Get Betty to validate your parking!"

The doors closed and the office was silent. Her pages were scattered on the table. She heard the massive old clock ticking from behind Ted Conway's enormous mahogany desk.

Her heart pounded in her throat. Linda O'Brien's cell phone rang, she looked at the display, blanched slightly, flipped it open, whispered "Hey, what's up?"

Sandy Folson said, "Hey, I need some money."

Linda O'Brien whispered back, "Again? This is starting to get weird. Why didn't you tell me the boxer character was based on a real person?"

Sandy Folson said nothing, and then replied, "Who cares? She dated my niece. I need more money."

Linda said, "I need to know where she's boxing next. My boss was at the ring, for the matches, and lost a lot of money. Now he wants inside information about future fights."

Sandy Folson said, "I'll ask next time I see my niece. Then I'll need even more money. Just another loan between friends."

"It's starting to seem like more than loans," Linda whispered, "Like if I don't keep paying, you'll do something."

Sandy Folson, asked, "Like what?"

She breathed deeply, looked around the office, and whispered, "Like if I don't pay, you'll tell my boss you wrote the girl boxing stories."

Sandy Folson laughed, "Well of course I will, silly girl. Why else would you keep lending me money? So get over here and bring me a bag of cash, the same amount as before, so I don't have to ask my attorney call their attorneys and set up a meeting. Duh, I'm not paid to write; I'm paid to keep my mouth shut. Jesus Christ."

Linda O'Brien was shocked by Sandy Folson's candor, "Uh, okay. Where, your house? With traffic, I can be there in an hour. Bye."

She pressed the button to end the call and closed the phone, stared at it in her hand, thought, "Cell phones rarely bring good news."

She stood, walked to the office doors and let herself out, searching for Betty to validate her parking.

Seven

Samantha Lucas sat alone on the hood of Esmeralda Ortiz's small car, more parking tickets pruned from under the worn windshield wiper blades and discarded, at the curb near a taco truck a block from the hospital eating tacos. She faced away from the white truck, looking up the hill, chewing greedily. Her escort from the hospital had been nice enough to tell her of the specialties at the taco truck around the corner.

Folks in scrubs and nurses' clothes and white coats were in line or standing around the shrubs near the sidewalk eating with friends and colleagues. Cindy Roberts tapped Samantha Lucas on the shoulder; Samantha Lucas spun half ready to fight, relaxed, smiled with strings of shredded cabbage hanging out of her closed lips, chewed her bite, and hurried to swallow.

Cindy Roberts said, "I thought that was you. You didn't get far."

Samantha Lucas confided, "I never pass a taco truck with a line. These are so good, what kind did you get?"

Cindy Roberts looked guilty, confessed, "Fried potato. They're tasty - and so fattening, how about you?"

Samantha Lucas held up a hand covered in dark red-hot sauce and dripping sour cream, "Fish. I always get fish tacos. I was in Baja once, near the shore and the fish tacos were amazing. This old man would literally catch the fish as you ordered and his son would cut the heads off, gut, skin, filet, batter, and fry them right there. Two corn tortillas, a little lettuce, some Pico de Gallo, a dash of hot chili sauce, and some radish slices: yum!"

She took another big bite, chewed and smiled.

Cindy Roberts told her, "I never got into the radish thing."

Samantha Lucas swallowed, said, "It's addictive. It's a soul food; they grow everywhere down there so everyone eats them. They also absorb the spice from the hot sauce cleanse your palate, just like with sushi."

Cindy Roberts retrieved her order from the taco truck guy when he called her name, excused herself from her colleagues, and sat with Samantha Lucas on the car's small brown hood in the sun and ate.

Cindy Roberts unwrapped her food, said, "I wish I could've seen you fight."

Samantha Lucas grinned, "Why, you like boxing?"

Cindy Roberts said, "No, no: too violent."

Samantha Lucas thought for a moment, and then told her "I guess I like the violence, it's kinda a violent ballet, but it's pure, free. Undisguised."

Cindy Roberts said, "Definitely undisguised. I think I prefer my violence a bit more passive or disguised, or not at all?"

Samantha Lucas looked at the pavement, and then said, "I already miss it. Funny."

"Would you have dinner with me sometime?" Cindy Roberts asked, feeling suddenly shy, feeling suddenly junior high, sounding suddenly awkward.

Samantha Lucas was shocked, "Sure, of course! Really?"

They stared at each other, and then she asked again, to confirm the stare, "Really?"

Cindy Roberts blushed a little, "Yes, really. Why not?"

Samantha Lucas laughed, happily surprised, "I don't know. You're just so -"

"Just so what? A smarty-pants girly-girl?"

Samantha Lucas stopped laughing, looked at her, whispered, serious, "No. Hot. You’re just so fucking hot."

Cindy Roberts grinned.

Samantha Lucas pulled her iPhone out of her jacket pocket, still serious, "You're sure? You're not scared of me after assaulting your intern."

Cindy Roberts told her, "I know crazy and I know violent and then I know situational behavior. I'm not scared. Well, maybe a little scared."

Samantha Lucas was suddenly scared too, "Text me your address."

Cindy Roberts pulled out her small cell phone and flipped it open so they could quickly text one another.

Later that night, illuminated by a bright moon and a cloudless, starless, Los Angeles night sky, Samantha Lucas rang Cindy Roberts' Studio City condominium doorbell. The wooden door opened, Cindy was dressed in post-work cocktail casual, and Samantha Lucas wore her trademark tracksuit,

Cindy Roberts said, "Hey, come on in. Any trouble finding me?"

Samantha Lucas crossed the threshold, looked around, "Nope."

Cindy Roberts asked, "Hungry?"

Samantha Lucas grinned, whispered, "Starving."

She gently rested a hand on Cindy Robert's shoulder, stood behind her, and kissed, bit, her warm neck. Cindy Roberts closed her eyes, leaned into Samantha Lucas, whispered, "Me too. We have reservations in an hour."

They turned toward each other and kissed slowly, deeply.

Samantha Lucas pulled away, whispered, "That gives us plenty of time."

Gently they explored each other. The feeling of another woman's body, like half the sensation of feeling her own body, was overwhelming in the sensation of self-exploration but without the flip side of choreographed accompanying body sensations. They gently worked to access each other completely.

Fabric covering excited skin they gently massaged and tugged away.

Elastic binding the coveted sections of each woman stretched tighter for fingers to gain access beneath.

Buckles pulled tighter by exploring hands they pulled loose from tongues of leather and flaps of fabric until released, granting the desired access.

Buttons keeping clothes in the way they fumbled with and popped out from their corresponding holes.

Zippers unceremoniously zipped while getting dressed they slowly worked back down, loosening teeth to give access to hungrier teeth.

Clasps, confining and frustrating, they struggled with and overcame by pulling still-clasped garments overhead.

On their knees, atop the pile of discarded clothes, pants balled around ankles, each played her tongue against the other's, they shared long breaths exchanged between lungs through deep kisses.

Samantha Lucas extracted Cindy Roberts' large breasts from her thick, lacy, loose-hanging bra and lowered her head to suck a single nipple hard, deep in her mouth, her hot tongue spinning slowly clockwise all the while. She ran the fingers of her right hand down the nearly naked woman's neck, back, belly, groin, bottom and thighs, spilling sensation across Cindy Roberts as she in-turn peeled the tracksuit pants down Samantha Lucas' waist and thighs.

Cindy Roberts' first-date bra-matching lacy boy-shorts joined the wadded pants around her knees and ankles. Samantha Lucas explored with one hand firm thighs and found the hair trimmed short in the shower just hours earlier. She effortlessly inserted her middle fingers deep into the now-grinding naked woman in the front hall of her home.

Cindy Roberts pinched Samantha Lucas's nipples, and slowly slid a hand down the boxer's back, under the thin elastic of her thong, the tight elastic rubbing the back of Cindy Robert's quivering hand as she felt down and around the curve of muscled buttocks, and inserted fingers into wet hairless warmth between parted legs, leaving her middle finger out to tease and press and rub beneath tight thong fabric pulled tighter.

Samantha Lucas and Cindy Roberts failed to cum together but each came hard, first Cindy Roberts then Samantha Lucas, grinding noisily with their knees planted firmly on the itchy front hall runner. It was a release both women needed: Cindy Roberts coming off a six-month dry-spell with no girlfriends and no serious dates, the batteries in her vibrator starting to wan.

Samantha Lucas needing a different warm body to erase the memory of Esmeralda Ortiz from her heart, her mind, and her body. Afterwards she realized the underwear she was wearing were a pair of Esmeralda Ortiz's. One of the now missing perks of dating someone her same size.

Lying on their backs, playing with each other's fingers, each woman studied in silence the white ceiling above. A small brown spider tracked a drunken upside down course above until it came to the brass base of the hanging hall light and disappeared. Cindy Roberts sat up, untangled her clothes, and started getting dressed. Samantha Lucas, on one elbow, hooked her bra for her, untangled her tracksuit pants from around her own ankles, and pulled her own clothes back on too.

Mellow and satisfied they left the condominium, eyelids heavy. They drove Cindy Robert's small Mercedes to dinner at the hip new Latin eatery, Tres Amigos Muertos. Seated at an outdoor table, curb within view, they ordered a pitcher of Jicama Margaritas on the rocks, salt-rimmed glasses, and a huge platter of tacos. They ate quickly, were drunk fast, and talked much longer than either intended; both wanted nothing more than to return to Cindy Roberts' condo to explore each the other further in her waiting bed.

They drank coffee. Their dinner remnants, the empty taco platter and assorted tasty crumbs, littered the table. Desert declined, their waiter left the check and cleared random empty dishes.

Cindy Roberts asked in a whisper, "They shot her?"

Samantha Lucas told her again, "On the ground."

Cindy Roberts again asked, "What did they do with her? I mean her body?"

It pained Samantha Lucas to admit, "I have no idea."

Cindy Roberts asked, "What about you? Won't they come after you?"

Samantha Lucas was confused, "Why would they come after me?"

Cindy Roberts looked incredulous, "Because you're a witness. Because if you can't fight anymore they have no need for you anymore. Because they might decide they want their money back, if you won't be taking anymore dives."

Samantha Lucas looked suddenly pale. They were the kind of guys who might change their minds.

Cindy Roberts pressed her, "What will you do now?"

Samantha Lucas shrugged, "I have no idea. I guess I should hide, maybe get out of town. I have no career, no place to stay, no future, except training. I need to find a legit manager. I have to become right-handed. None of that will help me if I'm dead or framed for murder. I guess I could box in prison, train in prison. It might lend me a little mystique?"

She smiled a little at her own small joke.

Cindy Roberts smiled a little too, said, "Believe me; you don't need any more mystique." She looked into her glass for answers, found none, drained it instead, and asked, "What do most boxers do when they retire?"

Samantha Lucas almost smiled, "I don't know. Fade away? Sell insurance? Or real estate? I don't want to retire. I don't want to leave town. I want to get better. I want to dominate."

Cindy Roberts said, "You could go back to school?" This was her father's general education-as-liberation solution for every crisis.

Samantha Lucas laughed, "Uh, no. School and I never really got along. I was thinking of going in partners on a gym I used to train at. The owner is a druggy and a gambler and always needs money so I figure if I buy-in and pull my weight maybe I can train some kids train my right. Help someone while I help myself reconnect with the legitimate women's boxing world."

Cindy Roberts brightened. Her own self-assurance had always made the indecision of others unbearable, "That sounds like a great idea."

Samantha Lucas said, "It's either that or write a screenplay."

They laughed and Cindy Roberts told her, "Yeah, me too; the L.A. condition: everyone has a screenplay for sale. In San Francisco, everyone has a web site for sale. My aunt Sandy writes for television and film. Its hard work; a lot of pressure. She makes a lot of money."

Samantha Lucas said, "Whatever I do it'll just be to keep from going back to the arena to ask the guys where she is. I know she's long gone by now I know no one will miss her. Her family decided she was dead when they met me." She flicked a small chunk of carne off the table with her fingertip, "Making people disappear is especially easy in L.A. I always figured all the hidden bodies around town had something to do with why there are so many rats everywhere." She picked up the check, laid out some bills, stood, "Let's get out of here."

Cindy Roberts, pushing her chair back, asked, "Back to my place?"

Samantha Lucas smiled, taking her hand, lacing their fingers, "Has to be; I don't have a place."

The two women kissed feverishly in the car, in the dark, in the parking lot behind the restaurant. Seated in the passenger seat, Samantha Lucas had the drunken doctor's pants and panties off and down on one foot in the blink of an eye. She maneuvered a warm, naked, right leg, with the clothes balled around the foot, up and around the passenger seat. Samantha Lucas turned, her legs in the gap before the passenger seat, and lowered her face down between the parted, smooth, bare legs, licking and nibbling wet folds of sensitive pink skin, before Cindy Roberts could utter a word of protest.

Cindy Roberts slipped into ecstasy after she pressed the button that locked the car's doors and then pressed the other button that moved the driver's seat back. Soon Cindy Roberts clenched Samantha Lucas by the collar of her tracksuit jacket and drove the boxer's face hard into her crotch, bucking and moaning with her own face pressed hard against the cold glass of the driver's side door.

As soon as Cindy Roberts relaxed, Samantha Lucas reemerged, smiling. She pushed Cindy's shirt and bra up over her large round breasts and alternated sucking each hard and bouncy nipple. Cindy pushed her away and rearranged Samantha Lucas so she was facing the back window of the little car, her waist stuck-fast between the leather front seats, a knee on either side of the center console, her hands clenching the retracted headrests atop the small back seat.

Cindy worked the tracksuit pants down and licked along the black elastic strap of the thong that disappeared in Samantha's bottom and emerged again over the pubic-bone tattoo. As she licked, she reached a hand up the inside of the tracksuit jacket and played with Samantha's dangling nipples while working the strap of the thong away to one side with her teeth. Then she inserted her tongue as deeply as she could into Samantha, while feathering the ABC's on her with a wet finger. Soon the car bucked and Samantha Lucas reached around and pulled Cindy hard by the hair, driving her face firmly into her.

They sat in the car in dark quiet breathing hard. Each disheveled and partially undressed. Their hurried breath completely fogged over all the little car's windows.

Samantha Lucas asked, "Are you okay to drive?"

At the condominium, they continued the process of getting to know each other's bodies. Late into the night, they ground on each other. Samantha Lucas lay splayed on her stomach on the mattress, covers and sheets and pillows all kicked off, legs wide, as Cindy Roberts lay on her belly on the boxer's back pinning her to the mattress, an earlobe clenched tight in her teeth, one hand snaked between them, down the crack of

Samantha's bottom and around, fingering her deeply from behind, her other hand sunk between the mattress and Samantha Lucas' pelvis, spreading the folds of her hairless skin open and pinching her roughly between feathery fingers. Samantha Lucas gyrated, bucked, and reached her good hand back behind both of them around Cindy Roberts' thigh, inserting her fingers into and tugging at the gentle folds between Cindy Roberts' scissoring legs. Bathed in sweat. The sheets on the mattress were soon soaked.

A week later Samantha Lucas and Cindy Roberts, wearing tank tops and boxer shorts, covered with blankets, lay in bed, in the dark, arm in arm, legs entangled, and heads on pillows facing each other, breathing each other, talking and whispering.

Cindy Roberts told her, "My parents already knew. We were always close and I never really had any serious boyfriends except the kind who don't know they're gay yet. So even on dates with boys in high school, not much happened. But on La Crosse field trips? Holy shit, the girls on the other teams were out. Big time. I was so distracted and horny I don't know how I ever scored a goal. Mostly I was so confused and baffled all the time."

Samantha Lucas asked, "Did you always know? I always knew."

"At the time I didn't," Cindy Roberts said, "because I didn't even know there was a name for it. Or that it was possible. Once I knew girls could be with girls, the hetero thing never entered my equations again. I told my Mom and Dad, and there was no looking back."

Samantha Lucas was amazed, "And they were cool? Are cool with it?"

Cindy Roberts was proud of her loving parents, "They're great with it. They always have been. They just always wanted me to be happy, want me to be happy. No matter what."

"That is fucked up," Samantha Lucas smiled in the dark, asked, "And so you've never even had a dick inside you?"

Cindy Roberts laughed, "Not a real one. Not one actually attached to a man."

Samantha Lucas could not believe it, "Not even in your mouth?"

Cindy Roberts laughed harder, "Not even in my mouth!"

Samantha Lucas asked again, "In your hand?"

Cindy Roberts told her, "In my hand all the time; burning warts off them or looking at lesions, always for work though. Yuck."

Samantha Lucas untangled herself from Cindy Roberts, turned onto her back, spoke to the ceiling, incredulous, "That's like a vegetarian making meatballs! Or sausages! Yikes! That is fucked up!"

Cindy Roberts jumped on her, straddled Samantha Lucas and told her, "I'm a vag-itarian."

Samantha Lucas laughed and mocked a fussy vegetarian's voice ordering in a restaurant, "Excuse me, is there any dick in this pussy? ' Cause I'm a vag-itarian!"

They tickled each other and tried to get into each other's shorts under the covers.

A few weeks passed and they slipped comfortably into domestic routines. Samantha Lucas had hidden almost all her money but insisted on paying for everything while jogging, and doing the laundry, and cleaning while watching daytime television while Cindy Roberts worked regular long hours at the hospital, her days off varying. One afternoon, Cindy Roberts post-call, they walked hand in hand down the street to do a little shopping, stopping into clothing stores along the way and looking for a place to buy Samantha Lucas new ear-buds for her iPhone.

"I need more normal clothes," Samantha Lucas said, looking into the window of a large clothing store.

Cindy Roberts laughed, said, "Oh my God, and here I was worried you'd always be one of those dyke-jocks who wears tracksuits for the rest of her life!"

Samantha Lucas smiled self-consciously, suddenly a little embarrassed by her dyke-jock uniform.

Cindy Roberts saw the embarrassment and changed the subject as they strolled along the sidewalk, "My fellowship starts next week. I'll only be gone for a month. If you want to stay at my place you can."

Samantha Lucas looked at the ground, "I don't know, are you sure?"

Cindy Roberts smiled, "Sure I'm sure. You practically live with me as it is."

Samantha Lucas looked at her girlfriend, "I know. I'll get my own place while you're gone. I'll be out by the time you get back."

Cindy Roberts stopped walking, held Samantha Lucas' hand tighter, "Sam. I'm not saying that. Just move in with me. Please?"

Samantha Lucas pulled her along, said, "I don't know, I have a lot going on in my head. I need to get back to my life. I need to stay involved with my training."

"Why are the two mutually exclusive?" Cindy Roberts asked. She held her hand tighter, "live with me, be with me, and get back into boxing too. With enough physical therapy, maybe I can help you get the strength back in your wrist. Maybe."

Samantha Lucas acquiesced, "Okay, maybe."

Cindy Roberts confirmed with a smile, "Maybe?"

Samantha Lucas repeated, "Maybe."

They walked together, arm in arm and trailed into an electronics store. Inside, a wall of massive televisions displayed a daytime soap opera. The employees of the store, mostly men, stood in a row watching.

Cindy Roberts recognized the music, said, "Hey my aunt Sandy - the one I told you about - is friends with the head writer of this show."

Across the wall of the store were two female boxers in a sparring ring wearing headgear and boxing gloves. As they circled each other, the shot dissolved to a scene of the same two women in bed, intimately talking. They told each other how they came out to their families. The sales team all smiled at the images of the sexy jocks half-naked in bed together. Samantha Lucas and Cindy Roberts watched with rapt attention.

Samantha Lucas squeezed Cindy Roberts' arm and whispered, "What the fuck?"

Cindy Roberts sat heavily down on a nearby leather home-theatre display chair and stared at the repeating wall of the women in bed, said, "I had no idea."

The two women in the store stared at the two women on all the televisions until a commercial for baby wipes interrupted their distraction.

Samantha Lucas said, "It's like watching me on television. How the fuck? You told your aunt about us? About me?"

Cindy Roberts was suddenly even more mortified, "Yes. Of course I did. Shit."

Samantha Lucas was baffled, "Why?"

Cindy Roberts told her, "Because that's what families do; they share about themselves with the people the love and are close to." She paused and thought it through, "And then my aunt Sandy must have told her friend about us, about you, and she wrote it up as a story-line now my life, your life, is on fucking television."

"Wait," Samantha Lucas, said, "You don't know that."

Cindy Roberts smiled, asked, "How many dyke boxers do you think there are in the world? In L.A? Dating women related to writers. In the television business? Friends with the writers of that show?"

"You're right," Samantha Lucas acquiesced.

"I'm sorry," Cindy Roberts told her, "It never crossed my mind in a million years. Are you so pissed?"

"Hell no," Samantha Lucas smiled, "I love it! I just want my cut. If I'm inspiring television writers I want to be paid!" She laughed, "There's a certain amount of hazard pay I should qualify for just living my life. If Esmeralda Ortiz's murder is gonna play out on television for the world to witness I might need to get paid extra, ya know? Can we have lunch with your aunt today? Would that be cool? And not keep shopping?"

Cindy Roberts was relieved; she did not want to lose her new girlfriend over a random, potentially huge, trust issue in which she was completely to blame.

"Yeah, sure, of course. I'll call her. Okay. Great. You're not mad? Oh my God; I'm mad."

"No, I love it," Samantha Lucas smiled, "The girl playing me is fucking hot. Maybe we could take her out for drinks!"

"Fuck you!" Cindy Roberts stood and clasp Samantha Lucas in her arms and they kissed as the wall of televisions resumed with the show, filling the store with repeating massive images of two happy women on every screen, arm-in-arm, half-covered, wrapped in bedding, sitting at the foot of the disheveled mattress, kissing deeply.

Eight

Linda O'Brien, convertible top down, pulled up to the curbside in front of a massive white house where the dark Suburban from the grocery store parking lot sitting in the driveway. Kid stuff littered the thick dark-green lawn. A small woman in big, dark, expensive sunglasses, Sandy Folson, wearing her pink nightgown covered by a light blue terry-cloth bathrobe, black China-flats with brown soles, and smoking a long, brown, skinny cigarette with a long cut-crystal high-ball glass, half-full of Bloody Mary and ice cubes in her hand, picked up random toys.

Linda O'Brien cut the engine, turned her music off, "Hey. Here."

She stuck her hand out holding a thick envelope, Sandy Folson crossed the sidewalk and the parkway and rested her drink on the car's hood, took the proffered envelope, pocketed it, reclaimed her drink, leaned against the English convertible, and smiled, "Thanks so ever much, you're saving my life! Need any new arcs? I have stacks of outlines, completely wrong for my other folk's shows, not going anywhere."

Linda O'Brien glared, "Sandy, you're fucking black mailing me. Why would I buy any more scripts from you?"

Sandy Folson was a little hurt, a little confused. Incredulous, looking at the broken toys and the drink in her hands, she said, "Because they won an Emmy. Because my stories are great! Because we're friends from college so long ago. This isn't blackmail, these are grants inspired by a fear of exposure. I wouldn't blackmail you; you're too good a friend. Is it pretty? Our Emmy?"

Linda O'Brien let herself be distracted like a child, forgetting for the moment that she was mad. She was thrilled to talk about herself, her achievement, "It's heavy. Heavier than it looks it fits in your hand just perfectly, like if your house was on fire or your yacht was sinking, you could clutch it without fail until you reached a safe distance or the Coast Guard fished you from the drink. I slept with it for the first week, tied little bows on it too sometimes it looks golden, but other times it looks silver, depending on the light, and she has nice detailing - wait, fuck you," she glared again, "you're a blackmailer."

Sandy Folson, tired of the lack of gratitude, said, "Well you're a fraud. So what? Welcome to Hollywood. Want a drink?"

Linda O'Brien looked at her watch, "It's ten in the fucking morning."

"So?"

Linda O'Brien acquiesced, "Yeah, okay."

She got out of the car, they walked up the sidewalk through the center of the yard, went inside the pristine Santa Monica house through the massive front door.

As they passed through the cavernous, ornate rooms inside, littered like the yard with random kid stuff, toys, teen books, exploded video game systems in tangles of wires near televisions larger than the children who lived there, Sandy Folson continued to pick things up as they walked, and kept them in her hand.

They entered the bright, modern, expensive kitchen and sat at the long granite island where a matching cut-crystal pitcher of Bloody Mary's sweated, waiting for them. Sandy Folson deposited her pile of plastic gadgets, broken little cars, and barrettes. She filled her own glass then poured a fresh drink for Linda O'Brien in another tall glass retrieved from a nearby cabinet with large glass doors.

As they drank the Bloody Mary's in silence, a Latino woman cleaned and washed dishes while a team of Latino men, visible through the floor to ceiling plate-glass windows, arrived to mow and blow the enormous back yard. Another Latino woman chased and chastised small kids as they careened through the house.

Linda O'Brien watched the back of the woman who washed the bizarre number of breakfast dishes, "They want more content that follows the Emmy plot line, the woman mob boxer."

Sandy Folson crunched ice, removed and folded her sunglasses and rested them on the slick counter top, "So give it to them, she's your character now."

Linda O'Brien looked at the tired woman next to her, played with the sweat on her glass, "Yeah, but what really happened?"

Sandy Folson looked back at her, "What do you mean? Sweetie, I actually made it all up. So I based it on a real character that boxes for the mob downtown. So what? I made up the rest. Who cares about the real person? We're writers: we earn a lot of money for telling intricate lies that the whole world enjoys. I don't know what happens next. Once the story starts the real inspiration no longer has anything to do with the lies; they become apples and oranges."

Linda O'Brien protested, "Yeah but..."

Sandy Folson rolled her eyes, "Oh come on Linda, it's all bullshit. What, you think my staff and I sit around swapping anecdotes from our lives or other people's lives to come up with story lines? That's not what you guys do in your writer's meetings, right?"

She looked away, that was exactly what they did.

Sandy Folson said, "That's what actors do when they play the "One Day I'll Be the Producer or Director" game, waiting around for their scene, playing cards with the other actors and below-the-line people while trying to keep their makeup from sweating off."

Linda O'Brien was embarrassed.

Sandy Folson continued, "Or reading the damned newspaper for stories? I just fired an assistant because I found out he subscribed to something like ten small newspapers from around the country he was actively mining "original" ideas from."

Linda O'Brien chuckled, mortified, feeling transparent.

Sandy Folson kept on talking, feeling drunk, "My clients could have been sued so hard. Jesus Christ, it only takes one hack somewhere out there to put two and two together, especially watching nationally broadcast shows, before someone's being sued for infringement or whatever."

Linda O'Brien bounced back, "My fucking Executive Producer was at her fights. He lost a lot of money on her fights. He figured it out. So cut the bullshit and tell me who she is because he wants to win his money back. Jesus Christ."

Sandy Folson smiled, "Ah. Well, uh, she's my niece's girlfriend they're on their way over here now."

"What?"

"Cindy called right after you. They saw the show want to talk. So I invited them over for lunch."

"Fuck."

They each took a long drink, crunched ice, said nothing. The lawn mowers buzzed outside.

The Housekeeper interrupted their silence, "Excuse me Miss Sandy, you want for me to make lunch for you and your friend and the kids?"

Sandy Folson raised her eyebrows, "And my niece Cindy and her friend are coming over too. Is that okay?"

Linda O'Brien looked into her glass, the day was shot, said, "I could eat."

The housekeeper smiled, asked, "You want maybe I make you some tacos?"

Sandy Folson smiled, "That would be great! Can you make enough for the four of us, and the kids, and you, and Consuela, and the guys outside too? They look hungry."

Linda O'Brien spoke to her glass, "Jesus, I love tacos."

Remembering the envelope of cash, Sandy Folson retrieved it from her robe pocket, "Oh yeah, I almost forgot, do we owe you for two weeks or three?"

The housekeeper, retrieving taco fixings, placing pots and pans on the spotless stainless steel range bigger than Linda O'Brien's car, and turning burners on, brightened, "Three weeks, Miss Sandy. Three weeks."

She counted out bills from the envelope, "I think we owe Consuela and the gardeners too," she made three small piles, "here's three weeks and here's next month too."

The housekeeper turned from the cutting board grinning, "I make a whole lot of tacos!"

Sandy Folson pushed one pile of cash across the wide counter top, the housekeeper scooped it up, Linda O'Brien watched, looked in her glass, drained it, she shook the glass, chomped ice.

Sandy Folson drained her glass too, "Another?"

Linda O'Brien agreed, "Yeah, fuck, why not? Holy shit, this is going to suck. When will they be here?"

Sandy Folson looked at the little platinum and diamond watch on her wrist, "Any minute." And poured fresh drink for them both.

They sipped the tall Bloody Mary's and waited for their guests. The kids ran through the kitchen and around their stools, chased by Consuela Robles, totally ignored by the two drunken writers. The doorbell rang; the housekeeper stopped her chopping, wiped her hands on her apron, and left the kitchen muttering.

On the other side of the large door, Cindy Roberts and Samantha Lucas waited. They stood in sun lit silence. Samantha Lucas studied the house, the yard with grass like a carpet and pristine installations of manicured shrubs and flowerbeds. She noted the empty tree-lined suburban street, with nannies on cell phones or manicured moms in workout clothes pushing baby strollers, and fashionable older Asian women walking slowly in pairs wearing large-brimmed straw hats.

The door opened and a short Latino woman in a light-blue maid's uniform smiled and gave Cindy Roberts a hug around her neck as she entered the house saying, "Renata, the door was locked!"

The small woman replied, "I know. I sorry. I forgot you're coming." She looked at Samantha Lucas, smiled, offered her hand, and said slowly in accented English, "I am very pleased to meet you."

Samantha Lucas took Renata Martinez's offered hand and said, "I am very happy to meet you too?"

Cindy Roberts laughed, said, "This is my friend Samantha. Wow Renata, you've been practicing!"

The small woman blushed, "You come to the kitchen, they're in there getting drunk."

"They? Who else is here?" Cindy Roberts asked.

"I dunno. Some writer friend of Miss Sandy's. Miss Linda?"

The diminutive housekeeper led them through the messy palatial home through room after room until they were in a kitchen that looked to Samantha Lucas like a Swedish resort or an expensive exercise club. Everything was white and steel and granite and clean and bright. Two middle-aged women sat at what appeared to be a massive square wet-bar. One woman wore a matching beige cotton tracksuit that would never see a minute of exercise and the other wore a ratty old blue bathrobe over a pink nightgown and funny black slippers. Each held onto a tall drink with a lonely stalk of celery swimming in tomato juice, ice, and liquor.

When the young women entered the kitchen, the two older women hopped off the tall stools and stood, Cindy Roberts said, "Hey guys! Look at you two; drunk and it's not even noon! I knew I should've become a writer!"

The women smiled and Cindy Folson said, "Well what the fuck do you expect from us? The kids are at school or here being looked after and we're prisoners of our creative powers."

They took turns hugging Cindy Roberts as Samantha Lucas stood and watched.

Cindy Roberts said, "This is my girlfriend, Samantha Lucas."

Samantha Lucas extended her hand and they took turns shaking it, "I am so happy to meet you!" Sandy Folson said, holding Samantha Lucas' hand in hers, "Cindy has told me so much about you!"

Cindy Roberts said, "Easy, she knows, she knows."

Linda O'Brien took Samantha Lucas' hand after Sandy Folson, shook it and said, "Oh, well than, we know so much about you. Have made up so much about you. I guess we have a lot to talk about!"

"I guess we do," Samantha Lucas agreed with a toothy grin.

Linda O'Brien asked, "You're not mad, are you? That we used you as the basis of a character?"

Samantha Lucas smiled, said, "I'm still a little freaked out by the whole idea, to tell the truth."

Linda O'Brien asked, "But you watch the show?"

Samantha Lucas looked uncomfortable, confessed, "Well, not really. Once when my grandmother was sick and she lived with us for a while when I was little, she and my mom watched it every day. For a few weeks. I don't think I've ever really seen it, otherwise, until this morning by accident."

Linda O'Brien sighed, "No one I know or meet watches my show. I know it sucks. I know everyone works. No one out here watches daytime television, I guess."

Cindy Roberts asked, "Maybe when it was new fewer women worked, so they had the ability to watch it every day?"

Linda O'Brien agreed, "Maybe, I guess that's a good point. You know, I donate a gift basket with stuff from the show in it every year for the silent auction at my kid's school. When they have their annual fund-raiser it turns out no one ever bid on it there's cool stuff in the basket: DVD's, t-shirts, our cook books, a jacket, hats, passes to the lot to watch live filming on-set, walk-on extra roles, and credits for lunch at the network's commissary."

She took a drink of her Bloody Mary; the three women watched unsure what to say, "I was so proud at first, of the show. Of its fame. It's legacy at the auctions I would stalk by, because you know, you can't help but monitor the bidding for the things you donated, and maybe try to drive the price up it used to go really high, really fast I was so proud of my work. Of my self-importance. After the divorce, I found out it was my now ex-husband doing all the bidding, making his writing look different, to make me happy."

She crunched ice cubes, the women were mesmerized listening Linda O'Brien's car wreck of a life narrated for them in the kitchen, "And now that we fucking hate each other, of course he never bids on them. No one does. I can't. I found them all, four years of donated baskets, unopened, dusty, still wrapped in

Excelsior, that clear wrapping stuff, in the closet in his office at the house after he moved out. Bastard: If I'd known all the great stuff he did for me, like that, when we were married, I never would have tried to run him over when I saw him with that big-titty blond bitch-whore half his fucking age. Ever think that the inevitable medical complications from silicon-implants might be a bit of fucking karma for all those firm-chested broads who used two pieces of unsportsman-like bait to lure away other women's husbands?"

They all stood in silence in the kitchen for a moment, smiling at her awkwardly. Linda O'Brien wiped a tear back from her eye, shook the ice in her glass, realized she was ranting, smiled, and said, "Yeah, me neither. Christ, I am drunk."

Sandy Folson patted Linda O'Brien on her back, "C'mon guys, let's sit in the dining room and work this out. No more Bloody Mary's for you, sweetie."

She took the tall glass from Linda O'Brien's hand, rested it on the island, and lead them to a long dining room just off from the kitchen with a shiny mahogany table that seated at least twenty people. The four women sat at the end closest to the kitchen where four places had been set on a cream-colored silk tablecloth that only covered the table where they were seated, heavy silver, thick white linen napkins, and tall cut-crystal glasses of cold water completed the place settings. Renata Martinez brought each woman a large plain white china plate covered with steaming soft tacos. In the center of the table was another cut-crystal pitcher, this one full of cold water, a small dish of chili sauce, a saucer of thin strips of Renata Martinez's beef jerky, a large bowl of pork-rinds, and a small bowl of lemon slices.

Samantha Lucas was overwhelmed with the traditional home-cooked meal, caught the small housekeeper gently by the wrist, said, "Thank you so much. I love tacos. Everything looks and smells fantastic."

She let go and the little woman smiled as she retreated to the kitchen to feed the kids, Consuela Robles, herself, and to send paper plates of food out to the gardener and his sweating crew of helpers.

They ate and Sandy Folson asked between bites, "But you have seen the show lately that's why you're here. As an aside, the numbers for the show are the highest they've been in twenty years. Even men, strait men, are watching now, setting their DVR's to record it during the day, to catch the story of the characters inspired by you and your girlfriend. Who may or may not be killed-off soon. Right Linda?"

Linda O'Brien chewed, wiped at her mouth with a thick clothe napkin retrieved from her lap, swallowed, gulped water from the tall glass, said, "Correct. The show is healthier than it's been in decades. Because of the girl-on-girl story arcs. No offense."

"None taken," Samantha Lucas said, smiling.

"I was gay for a year when I was at Brown," Linda O'Brien volunteered, "so it's not such a stretch for me to imagine the details."

"Of course," Samantha Lucas replied patiently, to the woman who was gay for a year in college. "When was that," she wondered, "nineteen-seventy-eight?"

Sandy Folson and Cindy Roberts ate in silence, listening to the women's exchange.

"And of course," Linda O'Brien continued, "the show did when an Emmy recently. A Daytime Emmy. For episodes featuring the woman boxer character."

"My character," Samantha Lucas asserted between bites.

"The woman boxer character," Linda O'Brien replied, and then took another bite of taco.

"The woman boxer character who fights in illegal prize-fights, in L.A, who eventually breaks her arm, whose girlfriend is eventually killed by the mob, who then eventually dates a doctor, and with her help trains for a comeback and eventually goes legit, and onto a wildly successful career, retires, and sells useless kitchen appliances on television?" Samantha Lucas asked smiling.

"Jesus Christ," Linda O'Brien muttered, "it's like she read my outlines for the next three seasons. Fuck. Well you have no legal way of stopping us from using the story."

Samantha Lucas laughed, raised her good hand over her plate, made a fist, joked, "If I wanted to stop you from using my story, I'd just stop you. Ya know?"

Linda O'Brien felt existentially sick. Like whenever she met with Ted Conway, her existence continued merely due to the will of another. She read of Harvey Teach's "suicide" in Variety earlier that week.

"I don't want to stop you," Samantha Lucas was telling her, "I want to help! Like I said in the kitchen, I'm still a little freaked out, but I love it! I want all those unclaimed gift baskets in your ex-husband's office closet. I want a jacket, and a hat, and DVD's of every season I ever missed. I want to see the sets and meet the actor playing me. I want to see your Emmy!"

Cindy Roberts punched Samantha Lucas in the arm, "If you get to meet her I'm coming too!"

"Okay, okay!"

"Holy shit, I thought you wanted us to stop," Linda O'Brien wiped another tear from her eye, "I thought you were mad now. You seemed mad to me. Hell yes you can help; I only have about a million questions for you! You can have all the fucking gift baskets! Of course you can come on the set; we can go right now if you like! I thought you might want money too. Jesus, what a relief."

Samantha said, "I do. I do want some money. How much is this all worth?"

Linda O'Brien stopped smiling, leaned back in the massive dining room chair that engulfed her, "Fuck. I knew it. Everyone wants money."

Sandy Folson fished the worn envelope of remaining cash out of her robe pocket, laid it on the table in front of Samantha Lucas, said, "See if this is enough."

Samantha Lucas picked the envelope up, opened it, took a quick count of the bills, put the envelope in her jacket pocket, and said, "Yeah. This is enough. Every month for the next twelve months?"

Linda O'Brien laughed, Sandy Folson said, "Every month for the next year; I'll pay you so there's no connection from Linda to you if her contract gets negotiated down, or she quits, or they fire her, or her residuals change, we renegotiate your cut. Agreed?"

Samantha Lucas smiled, "Agreed."

She and Linda O'Brien reached across the wide table and shook hands. Then they all ate in peace. Renata Martinez returned and piled more tacos retrieved from a heavy, smoking, steel skillet onto Samantha Lucas' plate.

Samantha Lucas told her, "Thank you so much. These may be the best tacos I ever ate in my whole life!"

Sandy Folson looked at her own empty plate, looked up at Renata Martinez, hurt, "what the heck, Renata?"

Renata Martinez smiled saccharine-sweet at her employer, "you on a diet, you remember?"

She left the dining room for the kitchen before Sandy Folson could protest.

Linda O'Brien said, "There's just one more thing. My boss, the Executive Producer of the show, lost a lot of money on your last two fights wants a chance to make it back."

Samantha Lucas chewed, considered this, swallowed, and said, "He wants a good tip? An inside connection? Tell him when I make my comeback, if I make my comeback, and go legitimate; to bet everything he has on me. On technical knock-outs in the first round of every one of my fights he'll never lose: I'm through taking dives, I'm finished holding back, and I'll never lose again."

She smiled and took another large bite.

Cindy Roberts agreed, "She's not kidding. I've seen what she can do. The woman is fast. Smart strong."

Nine

The sun was high in the sky as Samantha Lucas slept. Cindy Roberts emerged from the shower wearing a towel, drying her hair with another towel. She dropped them, pulled on clean panties and a bra from her underwear drawer. She sat at her desk and checked her email from a laptop near to the bed. Luggage piled in a corner. She disappeared back into the bathroom and used her loud screaming hair drier. As she blew her long hair dry, Samantha Lucas stirred, sat up, and looked around.

Cindy Roberts returned to the bedroom, "Good morning beautiful."

She gave Samantha Lucas a deep kiss, Samantha Lucas, bleary-eyed, asked, "Hey. Any coffee?"

Cindy Roberts pointed, "On the table next to you."

Samantha Lucas spied the laptop, "Can I check my email too?" Taking the coffee in hand, sipping, "How did you know I drank it black? The first time you made me coffee?"

Cindy Roberts read her email on the small flat screen, stood, then sat on the bed, "A dyke boxer? Please."

Samantha Lucas hefted the laptop onto the bed and typed while Cindy Roberts said, "I like it sweet and strong, like my women!"

"I like it black and bitter, like my soul!" Samantha Lucas replied.

"Check your email but don't close mine," Cindy Roberts told her, "just minimize it for me."

She leaned over and kissed her. Samantha Lucas checked her email, read, got up, went in the bathroom, and peed while Cindy Roberts sat on the bed and brushed her long hair.

From the toilet Samantha Lucas asked, "What are you up to today?"

Cindy Roberts said, "I have to go in and check on patients for a few hours. Want to have a late lunch in a bit?"

The toilet flushed, Samantha Lucas emerged drying her hands against her t-shirt, "Fuck, I almost broke my neck in there!"

Cindy Roberts brushed with her long hair with her head held to the side, said, "Yeah, it's slippery from that stupid shower door; the rubber trim that's supposed to seal it's thrashed."

Samantha Lucas snuggled back under the warm covers, told her, "I'll fix it while you're gone."

Cindy Roberts stood, returned to the bathroom, and came back into the bedroom brushing her teeth; Samantha Lucas closed her eyes and smiled to herself in comfort. Cindy Roberts returned to the bathroom, Samantha Lucas heard her spit and rinse her toothbrush. Then Cindy Roberts ran back to the bedroom and threw herself onto Samantha Lucas, they laughed, rolled around.

Cindy Roberts pinned Samantha Lucas' arms to the mattress, something she loved doing, knowing there was no way she could actually hold the muscled woman if she really wanted to break free.

Samantha Lucas smiled, "You smell minty!" She raised her head off the pillow, kissed Cindy Roberts, rested her head back on the pillow, and said, "Mmmm, you taste minty!"

They rolled on the bed and kissed some more, Samantha Lucas worked her hands into Cindy Roberts' panties, they ground a bit in their underwear, abruptly Cindy Roberts disengaged, hopped up, "Easy now tiger, I'm gonna be so late, I gotta get going."

Samantha Lucas threw a pillow at her, "You started it!"

She sat up, checked her email, sipped hot coffee, there was a yell and a crash from the bathroom, Samantha Lucas looked up, "You okay?"

Cindy Roberts said nothing.

Samantha Lucas said, "Cindy?"

Again no reply.

She got up, pulled her boy-shorts wedge out of her butt-crack, tracked back into the bathroom, and hollered, "Fuck!"

In the bathroom, Cindy Roberts lay on the slick tile floor in a heap, a thick dark pool of blood flowing from the back of her head where it hit the floor hard and split open. Samantha Lucas stood over the motionless woman; she felt Cindy Roberts' neck with her hand, found no pulse, felt her wrists, no pulse. She got on her knees, the pool of blood was suddenly everywhere, but she avoided stepping in it or disturbing it as she started to try to give the dead woman mouth-to-mouth. Blood bubbled from her nostrils and mouth. Instead of placing her mouth on the bubbled bloody lips, she freaked out.

"Fuck!" She screamed again, scrambling out of the bathroom back into the bedroom. She looked around. Fumbled Cindy Roberts' cell phone out of her bag, dialed nine-one-one and waited, breathing deeply. It was busy. She flipped the phone off, put it in her pocket. Found the cordless phone for the house on the desk, again dialed nine-one-one, waited, listened to the ringing, listened to the recorded message. Waited. Wiped a tear back in from her eye. Waited.

A nasal voice said, "Nine-one-one emergency."

Samantha Lucas stammered, "I slipped, I hit my head, I feel like passing out. I'm bleeding, I'm dying! Save me!"

"Ma'am what is your address, what is your name?" The operator asked.

"I don't know! I'm dying!"

She hung the phone up, pressing the button. Laid it on the desk. Looked at it resting on the desk. It rang and she looked at the caller I.D. It was the nine-one-one operator calling back. She sighed with a shudder all through her body. She began getting dressed and stuffed the few possessions she owned into the duffle bag hastily retrieved from the bottom of Cindy Lucas' massive bedroom closet. She returned to the bathroom to collect her toiletries.

She looked at the dead woman again, and willed herself not to cry, willed herself through the condominium, cleaning up, logging the computer off, doing the dishes. She ran back to the bedroom, picked up the cordless phone, and tossed it into the bathroom. Once everything else looked in order, once she was satisfied there was no trace of her left in the apartment, she approached and opened the front door. She adjusted the knob to confirm it locked the door behind her, opened it, and let herself out.

Samantha Lucas firmly closed the door and quickly walked down the long halls and out of the building complex, across and down the street along the curbside, and turned out of sight of the tall condominium building around the corner. Tears streamed down her face. She walked like a woman on a mission. Taco stands seemed to litter every storefront as she approached a bus stop. She looked over her shoulder; the bus was approaching, just a few lumbering blocks away.

She waited for it, standing on the curb. As she waited, she spied the front page of the Los Angeles Times in a paper box in a row of paper boxes. On it was Esmeralda Ortiz's picture, taken, apparently, a few years earlier, when she was a varsity high-school volleyball player, framed by columns of text.

Samantha Lucas tried to read the story but the bus pulled to the curb, stopped, and passengers threaded on and off between the paper box and her. She reluctantly boarded, looking over her shoulder for a last glimpse of the young Esmeralda Ortiz on the paper, paid her fair, took a seat, and then navigated to the newspaper's web site from her iPhone retrieved from her pocket as the bus pulled into traffic.

A crazy homeless man sat in the seat behind Samantha Lucas muttering to himself as she read the story of Esmeralda Ortiz's tragic disappearance from the loving bosom of her family into a world of violence and boxing and sexual deviance. It broke Samantha Lucas' heart and confused her. She thought of Cindy Roberts' warning about the men she boxed for and decided, now that it was apparent Esmeralda Ortiz's memory would not be permitted to rest peacefully, she needed to take measures to assure her own unmolested safety and continued survival.

A cell phone rang and Samantha Lucas ignored it.

It kept ringing and the crazy homeless man stopped ranting, leaned in close over the seat back next to Samantha Lucas, and said, "Hey honey-baby, yer telephone is ringing."

His breath was hot and smelled like rotten broccoli, she hissed, "Fuck off, dirt-bag."

He leaned back and began quietly ranting again, she fished Cindy Folson's cell phone out of her pocket, having forgotten it was there. She looked at the display when the phone stopped ringing she opened it. She maneuvered the settings, turning the displays off, turning the ringer and all other sounds off. She switched it to auto-roam and she adjusted the speakerphone settings. Then she pressed the button for voice mail and adjusted all those settings too.

The bus lurched to the curbside and Samantha Lucas hopped off. She walked around the corner, down the street, and went into the doors of a gymnasium.

She said, "Hey," to the guys near the door who were busy pouring over racing forms and did not look up.

She passed into the main room where trainers and contenders worked bags, shadowed, did sit-ups and push-ups, and sparred in a few large boxing rings wearing headgear.

Anita Martel, the gym-owner's granddaughter, a pretty jock girl who was helping train some straggly-looking little kids with their footwork saw her and told them all to take five.

"Hey stranger! Where you been?" She hugged Samantha Lucas, "Terry and I almost gave up on you! Dude, everyone's looking for you."

Samantha Lucas smiled, "Dude, I had to stay the fuck out of Dodge for a while. We're cool though. Is she here?"

"Yeah, she's here," Anita Martel said, "Until everyone leaves and I lock up. Then she'll go back to fucking la-la land.

Samantha Lucas asked, "Still with that shit? What the fuck?"

Anita Martel said, "You ever think that grown up's who can't drop their bad habits are just weak little babies? Pussies?"

Samantha Lucas smiled, "All the time."

They laughed and slapped five, Anita Martel called her students back from the drinking fountain, "Come to the bar later. Terry's closing tonight."

Samantha Lucas said, "Yeah, I'll be there. Save me shot."

She threaded her way through the action of the busy gym and found the owner, a decrepit and sinister-looking old biddy, paying bills in her mean little faded military green office.

Samantha Lucas stood in the doorway, said, "Hey."

The old woman looked up, ignored her, and looked back down.

Samantha Lucas asked, "What?"

Mary Louise Martel kept writing checks, did not look up, and told her, "You got a lot of neck coming here after what you did to her."

Samantha Lucas was shocked "Wha? What? I didn't do anything to her!" She insisted.

Mary Louise Martel put her pen in its cap. Leaned back, looked the young woman in the eyes, said, "Arena physician said you cracked her skull, killed her then you just disappeared. Like a guilty coward now here you are. Folks are looking for you."

Samantha Lucas held her hands up, asked, "Bobby McGarry and Eddie Holleran's doctor said I killed her?" She shook her head, "that's not what happened."

Mary Louise Martel studied the young woman's face, "well that's what Bobby McGarry, and Eddie Holleran say happened."

She lit a skinny brown cigarillo.

Samantha Lucas entered the office, shut the door, sat down, said, "Fuck you old woman, I loved her. They fucking shot her in the head now they're blaming me? I broke my fucking hand and may never box again, lost my girl and my career, and now apparently I've lost any kind of friend in you I ever thought I had? Thanks for believing in me once, bitch."

She stood up to leave but Mary Louise Martel grabbed Samantha Lucas by her cast, looked at it, kept the young woman from leaving, "I didn't really believe them. Anytime crooks confide in you, it's just to cover their own misdeeds. You know that?"

Samantha Lucas pulled her fractured arm free, relaxed just a little, and asked, "Do you know where she is? Did they tell you where her body is?"

The old woman shrugged, "Off Long Beach Harbor. Eaten by the fishies by now. They own a deep sea fishing boat and keep her in a slip down there. They probably chopped her up and used her for bait. They have in the past." She studied her hands, and then looked at the cast on Samantha Lucas' arm, "is that true? And you're done?"

Samantha Lucas sighed, studied the sparring partners in the practice rings through the dirty office windows, "I came here to try to buy part of the gym from you, to become a trainer. To give other young kids a chance to train. To learn to lead with my right to give my left time to heal."

She pulled a white sock full of money knotted with rubber bands out of her duffle bag, fingered the cotton brick firmly, and placed it on the desk.

Mary Louise Martel looked at it, "They said you robbed them too. I couldn't figure how you could've gotten to the money since they keep it in a place you probably don't even know about."

Samantha Lucas told her, "This was my pay-off. For diving in that last fight."

Mary Louise Martel nodded, asked, "It was pretty obvious you could have taken her, even with just your right. She always has been more mouth than muscle. How much is in there? Is that a clean sock?"

Samantha Lucas and lied, "Yes of course it's clean. Mostly clean. I dunno, I haven't counted it."

Mary Louise Martel accepted the lies, "Well you can't stay here. There's no telling who might be dropping a dime on you out there right now. Go out the back and head somewhere you shouldn't be. I'll call you in a few days, shouldn't be too long; no body no crime we'll make you a trainer. So you can liberate all the young bums you like."

Samantha Lucas sighed, "Part owner."

Mary Louise Martel glared at the woman across the desk from her, "I don't need a partner."

Samantha Lucas sighed, "Fine. Never mind. Trainer. Jesus."

Mary Louise Martel repeated, "Trainer."

Samantha Lucas said, "I've been hiding for weeks. Can you keep the money for me? I only need a little bit of it. I need some real sleep and a shower; I'll go get a room at the No-Tell-Motel down across the street."

She untangled the rubber bands, took a few bills from the sock, twisted the rubber bands back around the white cotton and elastic sock, and held it out to Mary Louise Martel, who raised her hands in protest, "I don't want your money! What if something happens to you?"

Samantha Lucas glared at the old lady, "Just put it in the safe for me, please? I can't relax when I have it. It's blood money now. It's brought me no happiness. I'm sick of it. I'm tired."

Mary Louise Martel acquiesced, "Okay, okay. I want us to count it together first."

Again Samantha Lucas removed the rubber bands, unfolded the sock. Then extracted and laid the bills out in piles of one hundred dollars. Soon stacks of bills covered the old leather blotter and the sock was empty. They counted the money, then she made a loose brick of the piles and stuffed it back in the sock, smoothed them out into a flat unfolded, unbent pile, wrapped the rubber bands around again and handed the little white bundle to the old lady who turned and, leaning down from her creaky old wooden desk chair, entered the combination on the keypad of the shiny red, push-button safe with an electronic lock behind the desk. The keys beeped and she opened the door with a jerk of the handle, and rested the sock on a shelf among piles of envelopes and documents. She shut the door and entered the code again, then tried the handle confirming the unflappably tight locking of the safe.

Samantha Lucas left through a door in the back of the office, iPhone in hand, pressed against her ear. Mary Louise Martel finished writing checks and making entries in the large old ledger book on the desk, stood, picked up the receiver and deposited change fished from her faded jean's pocket into the pay phone on the wall near the office door, dialed, waited.

"Yeah, hey, it's me. She just left here through the back," Mary Louise Martel told the person on the other end of the line, "She's getting a room at the motel across the street. Naw, she wouldn't tell me what she did with the money. Probably has it on her. Will do. Okay."

She hung the receiver up with a crooked finger, burped under her breath. Studied the unmoving prizefighters from decades past, photographed and framed and hung on the yellowing walls, who stared at her, smiling, with their feet scissored apart and gloves raised, hair perfect, watching her every move from their graves. She put her thick glasses on, picked a scrap of paper up off the desk, extended it back and forth until she could decipher the scribbled black writing, removed her finger from the telephone, held the receiver to her ear again, deposited more change, dialed, and waited.

Mary Louise Martel cleared her throat, said, "Hey, it's me. I wanna come over and get a bottle."

Ten

Samantha Lucas emerged from the disused door at the back of the gym into an empty alley littered with garbage and discarded shipping crates, trash bins, piles of sodden cardboard once brown, and stagnate puddles of stinky brown water pooled in holes of broken asphalt with rainbows of oil dancing across their reflections. She walked the length of the alley, still listening to her iPhone, looked both ways at the busy cross street, sprinted across the four lanes of traffic through a gap made by the lights, onto the alternate curb and sidewalk and into the corner parking lot to the small office of the sleazy corner motel.

The door made a ding-dong chime sound when opened; Samantha Lucas stood feeling conspicuous until an Indian-American woman in a long pink and gold sarong and with a red dot on her forehead approached the Formica counter from a long skinny hall that accessed a living area through a jarred door. The office smelled of curry, old oil, and fried Samosas. The woman wiped her hands on a blue and white checked dishtowel and asked, "May I help you today?"

Samantha did not look like the usual whore or runaway requiring a room during the middle of the day.

She said, "I need a room for a few days. A quiet room away from other, uh, working guests."

The motel clerk looked at her and said, "Yes of course you do. Forty dollars per day and night. The Triple-A discount if you have the Triple-A membership. You have the Triple-A membership?"

Samantha took the fold of bills from her tracksuit pocket and peeled off a week's worth of room, smiled and told the beautiful woman who looked like a Christmas tree in the foyer of a synagogue, "Lady I don't even know what that is."

The woman smiled back and told her, "For the automobile. For your automobile."

Samantha Lucas told her, "I don't have a car."

The motel clerk eyed her suspiciously, "How do you not possess an automobile in the greater Los Angeles area? How do you navigate the numerous daily South-Land SigAlerts?"

Samantha Lucas grinned again, "I walk or ride the bus?"

The motel clerk thought about this, and then asked, "How am I to discount your room to the Triple-A membership rate if you have no Triple-A membership, and you have no automobile?"

Samantha Lucas asked, "Why do I need a car to get a room?"

This caused the motel clerk think, pursing her full red lips and looking at the small white card she wanted to fill out with a felt-tip pen she now held in her hand.

, "I do not know. It is what we do. I myself do not drive; I too have no Triple-A membership. So I will give you the Triple-A membership discounted room rate even though you possess no automobile and do not have the Triple-A membership."

She smiled, so pretty she distracted Samantha Lucas' preoccupied heart a little.

Samantha Lucas smiled too, confused by the difficulty in getting a scummy motel room. The clerk filled in the white card, took the cash, made change, and handed Samantha Lucas a large brass motel key connected to a large green disk of plastic stamped with a different motel's name and spray-painted a varying shade of green then scrawled upon in black permanent marker in large block lettering the motel's current name; REST LAND MOTOR MOTEL LA CA.

Samantha Lucas pocketed the key and key ring, shouldered her duffle bag, said "thank you," exited the small office watched by the clerk who stood, watching Samantha Lucas across the parking lot as she walked to the motel room door, with her dark beautiful eyes. Samantha Lucas slipped the key in the locked silver doorknob, shouldered the orange door open, entered the room, and disappeared. The clerk put the cap back on the felt-tip pen, returned it to a coffee mug full of similar, capped, felt-tip pens, and returned herself down the small hall to her waiting unwashed and undried dishes.

In the dingy room, Samantha Lucas spread her things, clothes, extracted from the duffle bag, haphazardly across the tops of the tired wood veneer table in the front window and atop mismatched dressers. She pulled back the polyester coverlet, studied the yellowed white cotton sheets, felt them with a hand, they were sandy. She rumpled the bed, bounced on it with her knees, and punched the pillows leaving them disheveled. She then removed her tracksuit, left it in a pile on the floor, kicking off her sneakers and socks as she walked to rear of the room and into the bathroom wearing just her underwear, a pair of blue panties and a black sports bra.

She started the shower, sat on the cold toilet and peed, watched her reflections in the large wall mirror over the vanity disappear in steam as the hot shower filled the small room with thick vapor. It billowed from the bathroom door she left slightly ajar. In the room, she had also left the front door ajar. Eddie Holleran had no problem slipping in and closing it tightly shut as the shower head sprayed loudly, obscuring Samantha Lucas from hearing his careful entrance. He studied the bed, studied the possessions hastily arrayed about the dressers and table, failed to spy the bags of money he and his partner now regretted giving her.

Eddie Holleran stood outside the bathroom door listening to the woman wash her hair. He recognized the sound of thick suds rinsed from a woman's head, splattering the shower floor, of the thin bathtub. He took a breath and slowly removed the holstered pistol and silencer from under the arm of his brown sports jacket, the same pistol he shot Esmeralda Ortiz with, and pushed the door further open with the toe of his shoe. He raised the long, blue, metal tip of the gun, leveled it, and studied the shower curtain.

Emptied ejected shells bounced off the door and the tile wall and ricocheted with little pings from multiple bounces as he pushed to door open further and quickly unloaded the pistol's magazine. Finished firing, he waited for the shells to come to rest. The curtain billowed. He pushed it aside with the extended muzzle of the gun but the shower was empty save all the sudsy towels and bath rags and floor mats piled in the bottom, making the shower sound occupied, and the eleven small holes in the shattered tile wall.

He turned to leave the hot bathroom just as Samantha Lucas, still in just her underwear, rolled from under the empty bed, rounded the doorway, and punched him square in the nose with the right jab of her carefully taped fist, collapsing his face, killing him instantly, and sending his fat body flying against the far wall where it fell and came to rest with the bloody remains of his nose and toothy jowls lodged fast against the filthy urine-soaked base of the steam-sweaty toilet.

Samantha Lucas cradled her right hand, taunted the dead man, mocking him, "What the fuck? Did I hit you Eddie? I must think you're some fuckin' girlie I can beat on."

She shook the pain out of her now-sore hand, stood over him, stooped, and began going through his twitching body's pockets as its muscles relaxed and a pool of urine darkened his slacks and the stench of defecation reached her nostrils, "I was holding back but should have kicked your ass first time I had the chance. Dick."

As she spoke to the deceased Eddie Holleran, she fished the cell phone from his pocket. She sat on the carpet in the room just outside the bathroom and looked through his received call log. Seeing a number she recognized from the gym, she deleted all the logs. Then brought up the photos on her iPhone, scrolled to a picture of Esmeralda Ortiz, dead on the locker room floor, and took a picture of the picture on her iPhone with Eddie Holleran's cell phone. It took a few tries until she was satisfied. She deleted the rejects. She studied the winner again. Closed the phone, and held her nose as she returned it to his jacket pocket. She ran her right hand under cold water and had trouble finding her reflection in the foggy mirror. She turned off the tap, shook the water off her wrist, maneuvered the knob turning off the shower, switched off the light, and shut the bathroom door, kicking the dead man's huge feet out of the way as it closed.

Samantha Lucas slept under itchy covers on a rigid motel room mattress. The lights of a Los Angeles evening played outside, shadows danced across her face. She stirred as she heard something. Bobby McGarry unloaded his shiny, black, silenced pistol into the shadowed bed he stood beside, feathers flew, shells bounced onto the scratchy blankets and short industrial shag carpet around his feet. After he unloaded the entire magazine into the limp mound on the bed, he poked the lifeless lump through the covers with the extended muzzle of his gun.

As he pulled a pillow out from under the blankets, Samantha Lucas, still in her underwear, rushed at him from the shadows, and drove her freshly re-taped fist into the shooter's face, crushing the front of his skull as she had his partner, killing him instantly. The big, tough man's carcass flew against the thin mint-green painted wall and worn nightstand, collapsing into a heap across the head of the bullet-riddled bed.

Samantha Lucas stood at the foot of the bed, shooting pain from her hand exploding in her eyes and singing an unholy aria in her ears. She studied the body. Watched it seep. Reveled in her revenge. In her freedom from bad men. In her power and her pride, in her strength, her agility, and her control. The sensation of death caused by her own power was an orgasm collected solely in her mind she grinned a little in the dark stench of the Triple-A-membership discounted motel room where she had executed two grown men.

Samantha Lucas collected her things into the duffle bag. She sat on the foot of the bed and unwrapped her stiff, swollen right hand, wrist, and the base of each finger. She wound the black ribbon into a tight spool, dropped it into the duffle on the floor, reached and picked up her tracksuit, straitened the slacks and sleeves, put her feet in the waste, stood, pulled on the jacket, zipped it and shouldered the bag. With a clean white sock pulled over each hand, she retraced her activity in the room, wiping her few fingerprints from as many surfaces as possible, she hoped.

She opened the motel room door, hung the DO NOT DISTURB sign on the knob, confirmed it was indeed locked, closed the door tight, flipped the funny metal slide-lock mechanism that replaced a chain lock at some point in the door's life, as indicated by extra screw holes and the small grooves from the links of a hanging chain that had been painted over. She returned to the adjoining room through the jimmied doors. She re-locked each in turn and made the bed in which she had been hiding. Then slipped out the front door, pulled it locked, put her hands in her pockets fingering the sock off each, and crossed the parking lot, eyes to the ground.

Moments later Samantha Lucas stood at a curbside pay phone a block from the motel. She ate from a folded paper plate of just-purchased tacos. She lifted the receiver, punched in nine-one-one, and waited. The phone rang and a recording asked that she remain on the line. She chewed and wiped at her mouth. As she waited, eating, an L.A.P.D. patrol car cruised past and she reconsidered what she was about to confess. She hung up the receiver, turned, and walked down the busy Studio City sidewalk.

Long after dark, Samantha Lucas returned to the silent alley behind the gym and slowly worked the lock of the back door. Eventually something mechanical clicked and she managed to get the cylinder to turn. She slowly exhaled. Samantha Lucas entered the dark hall, pulled the door closed, flipped the stiff brass butterfly handle of the dead bolt locked, and quietly stalked down the dark deserted hall.

She ascended the old stairs quietly after kicking her shoes off at their base. Atop the landing, she turned a corner and spied cautiously around a yellowed doorjamb into the gray living quarters littered with professional boxing memorabilia. As full as it was, with tired furniture, with dusty surfaces, and forgotten newspapers, book, and magazines, it felt empty, hollow. She entered the little living room and stood near the wall. Her view extended to the rest of the cramped apartment.

She hid in shadow, counting her shallow breaths, as the figure of the hunched old woman, Mary Louise Martel, walked to and fro, cupboard to cabinet, framed in the kitchen doorway and illuminated by a yellowed old single bulb as old as the old woman, hanging from a cloth-wrapped cord and switched by an old brass ball-chain, centered above the rectangular linoleum table. Eventually the old woman ceased her preparations and came to rest, heaving herself into a pitiful little wooden folding chair that had forgotten how to fold. She sat in the chair and faced the dark of the room where Samantha Lucas watched, facing the dark of the life around her, unaware of the girl in the shadows. She ignored the dark, ignored the rooms, the life around her, as she had for so many years, and tallied the precious possessions, common in every life, but special in hers, on the table before her: a chipped white shallow bowl, a small brown glass bottle, and a large soft green cotton towel.

As Samantha Lucas watched, the old woman unscrewed the little metal cap, poured a short thin stream of clear liquid into the bowl from the little brown bottle, screwed the metal cap back on, swirled the liquid in the bottom of the bowl, unfolded and spread the green towel over her head and arms as she bent over the bowl, making a tent over herself and the bowl, and proceeded to inhale deeply, slowly, the green tent gently, slowly, rising and falling.

As she carried out this ritual of selfishness, Samantha Lucas felt a tear sneak out from each of her eyes, and let them fall unencumbered down her cheeks. Another dead end life, like a sailor lost at sea whose heart-broken family could not help but continue to toss hopeful bottles stuffed with emotional pleas into the bay in hopes of one day reaching the missing. No idea if they were alive or dead, but less a family, each less an individual, for not knowing and for the emotion they squandered on unrequited familial hope; yearning wasted on fruitless love.

She snuck into the old kitchen, stole across the filthy linoleum floor, and stood in shadow behind the towel-covered old woman, as comfortable now with her adopted mantel of the angel of death as the old woman was under the towel, her face enveloped in fumes of earthly freedom. As velvety fingers of intoxication clasp her being in their gentle grasp, the deep inhaling eventually slowed and evened into shallow, gentle breaths. The towel fell from the dowager's shoulders as her head rose a little then lowered and came to rest, high as a kite on ether fumes, passed out, snoring gently, drooling, a fat pale cheek on the cold hard table.

Samantha Lucas retrieved the drooping towel from around the old woman's hunched backside, used the corners of it in her hands to grasp and unscrew the bottle's little cap, and poured the remaining ether in a thin stream into the shallow bowl, returned the bottle and cap to the table. She let the towel fall again, gingerly picked the old woman's surprisingly heavy head up by her gray hair, and gently rested it, face down, in the bowl of intoxicating liquid.

She stepped back again, hiding from the deed in darkness, listening to the bubbles sputter methodically with each slowing breath, watching without remorse as the old woman slowly overdosed and drowned.

Moments later, peaceful demise complete, Samantha Lucas stole back downstairs, found her shoes, and left the quiet rear domestic area for the gym, located the office, and sat in front of the big red safe. She smoked in the dark. She listened to her iPhone; the voice mail recording from the small cell phone in the sock in the safe with the stack of dive money ran long, and it took time to find the exact location of the code being entered. She placed the handset on speakerphone and listened to her conversation with the dead woman. The keys sounded clearly between muffled movements of the sock rubbing the cell phone's tiny built-in microphone. She hit the key to rewind, raised the volume, and punched the keys on the safe repeatedly until the tones she heard from her finger-stabs matched the tones coming from her iPhone, and the handle moved, clicked, and the thick little door swung wide. Exposing the sock, myriad stacks of money and packet upon packet of papers that appeared boring and financial or official for the successful continued running of any small business.

Samantha Lucas retrieved the small phone from the sock of money in the safe, stuffed it into a jacket pocket. She retrieved the small metal-shaded lamp from the desk, rested it on the ground near the open safe, and switched it on. Then she sat on the floor, legs crossed, facing the safe, and looked through the papers, sifting each stack with care, absorbing the unremarkable history and secrets of the gymnasium business.

An hour later, after slipping back out the alley door and taking the time to lock the dead bolt with her little black and silver lock-picks, she was walking down the sidewalk toward the bar around the corner. An angled row of old black motorcycles were parked, back wheels to the curb, in front of the bar with a large round black cartoon cat-face with thirteen's painted in the center of each eye instead of pupils, the address of the bar being thirteen-thirteen Los Gatos Avenue. The name of the bar was, cleverly enough, Thirteen Cats.

They talked about One-thousand-three-hundred-thirteen-cats as a name, but decided it lacked the same sinister ring as Thirteen Cats. The owner's girlfriend at the time he took over the building's lease from the previous proprietor had opposed the name because she was deeply into numerology and astrology and insisted the number, while sinister and cool, was still unlucky and summed unpleasantly in the worlds of numerology and astrology.

To which Terry Whitehead, the new proprietor in question, had replied, "That's the whole fuckin' point, darlin'."

Then he proceeded to get a matching black cat's-face with a large thirteen in each eye tattooed on each of his wide flabby biceps to compliment all the other tattoos he already had.

This had been when she broke up with him because, "Any man so immature as to want unlucky numbers etched into his skin, tempting the fates and upsetting the numerical balance of his chakras," she reasoned, "was too silly to date seriously."

The front of the building was painted glossy black, windows, and all, the sidewalk festooned with cigarette butts. The front door was recessed and the black walls littered with years of fliers for bands around town and coming soon to the Thirteen Cats' small stage.

Inside was smoky and music played from a jukebox regardless of whether or not a band was playing. It only contained seventies, eighties, and nineties punk, hardcore, old ska, and psycho-billy-cow-punk and played in an order controlled by two toggle switches screwed to the underside of the bar, near a three-foot length of heavy three-quarter inch galvanized pipe and a loaded thirty-eight pistol.

"Fuckin' misdemeanor charge for an unlicensed handgun is worth the fine if it means saving my fat hairy ass," Terry Whitehead was fond of saying to anyone who would listen.

Samantha Lucas paused a storefront away, pulled Cindy Lucas' small cell phone out of her pocket, removed the battery cover, battery, and little data card. She dropped the battery and cover into the curbside street drain, snapped the data card in half, placed the hollowed handset on the curb and stomped on it until the delicate little electronic bits inside the plastic shell splintered out like silicon guts. She then kicked the remains of the hand-held device and data card down into the same watery sewer-grave as the battery and cover.

Inside patrons in leather and denim drank and threw darts or shot pool. Anita Martel sat at the bar, alone, talking to Terry Whitehead, the short, three-hundred pound bartender and owner of the Thirteen Cats, once all muscle in another life, now all aspiring chef.

He smiled when he saw Samantha Lucas and called out to her in his scratchy, faded, ex-Texan drawl, "Sammy darlin', I just heard you were back among us. Get on over here and have a drink. Hell, I'll have one with you. Anita?"

Anita Martel downed the rest of her beer and Terry Whitehead poured three shots of cheap brown liquor for them. With a church key on a small-linked chain attached to a leg of the bar with a Phillips screw, he opened three brown bottles of cheap light beer retrieved from an ice-filled sink below the bar. They chinked the little shot glasses and each took a moment to drink the hot, fiery liquid. It burned and warmed each belly.

Samantha Lucas slapped the fat man on his shoulder across the bar, said, "I missed you Terry! How'd we do?"

The big man grimaced, mocked pain, "Holy Christ little girl, don't break my arm now, I got a whole night here to get through yet!"

He bobbed and weaved his massive frame as she took mock-shots at him, each time connecting to Anita Martel's zipped black leather jacket instead.

"We did alright, Sammy. We surely did all right. I heard what happened to Esmeralda," he turned the key in the drawer of the cash register, removed it and dropped it into a cavernous jean's pocket, motioned the two women to follow him through the crowd to the back of the bar, leaving a skinny bar-back flirting with drunk patrons in charge.

Through a door and into the quiet of his office they sat, Terry Whitehead behind a small desk piled with stacks of random papers and unpaid bills. Leaning back in the squeaking desk chair in fear for its life, he fished different keys from a different pocket. He unlocked a desk drawer and produced four rectangular bricks wrapped in gray newspaper. Anita Martel checked the office door to assure it was indeed locked, and Samantha Lucas unwrapped the bricks: each contained a four-inch tall stack of one hundred dollar bills tightly wrapped in plastic wrap, each with a single initial written on top: T, J, A, S.

"I sure am sorry 'bout Esmeralda," Terry Whitehead said between drinks of his beer. He smiled as he watched Samantha Lucas' face brighten at the sight of the money. "She was a nice woman. A good girl."

Anita Martel drank her beer too, looking at the four little skyscrapers of cash, said, "She was a good fighter a good kisser."

Samantha Lucas smiled, raised her bottle, they tapped them together, over the desk of disheveled newspaper, she said, "To Esmeralda Ortiz, a good fighter, a good kisser, and a good friend."

They drank in silence, a small fan on a filing cabinet oscillated across Terry Whitehead's constantly sweating frame. The office seemed smaller than when they sat down, the money on the desk taking up most of the room now.

Samantha Lucas said, "Who is the J stack for?"

Terry Whitehead looked closer, "That's an E. For Esmeralda."

Samantha Lucas looked again, "That's an E? It looks like a J."

Terry Whitehead smiled, "It's a sloppy E."

"I swear it looks like a J. Not an E." Samantha Lucas insisted.

Anita Martel interrupted, "Who cares what it looks like? Let's cut up her share; she's gone, and we're clear, and she won't need this now."

Terry Whitehead studied the wiry little lethal fighter and said, "Hell Sammy, Anita and I almost cut both your shares up last night. Good thing you showed up."

Samantha Lucas repeated, "Good thing."

Anita Martel put a calming hand on Samantha Lucas' arm, and told her, "We thought you were dead too."

Terry Whitehead and Anita Martel smiled, Samantha Lucas did not smile back, but she said, "I needed to be out of sight. I told you I would. I got distracted but now here I am. Ready to be back with you guys and ready to train."

"Well whatever her name was I hope you had fun," Anita Martel smiled a funny grin, "and I hope you're ready to start your own gym; I spoke to grandma last week about selling a stake and she said no way."

Samantha Lucas acted surprised, "when I talked to her today she took my money, told me the combination to the safe, and shook hands with me like it was a done-deal."

She took another drink from the beer bottle in her hand, started looking for a cigarette.

"Holy shit, no way!" Anita Martel exclaimed, "That's fantastic. Really? Told you the combination to the safe? She never told me the combo to the safe."

"She had to; she has my money locked in it. In a dirty sock."

They all laughed, Terry Whitehead took a large pocket knife from another drawer in the desk, sliced open the one brick of cash with his sloppy J written on it, and began dividing, counting out three additional short-stacks next to the three remaining bricks.

As he counted he said, "Who the hell knew just two fights could be so profitable?"

Samantha Lucas and Anita Martel smiled, Anita Martel said, "Terry, everyone knows boxing is profitable. That's why it's been around since ancient civilization."

Terry Whitehead stopped counting, said, "Well yeah, I guess ever since there's been more than two fellas and a good looking girl around, there's been fights, huh?"

"The Greeks were betting on pugilists long before the Romans ever hassled Jesus Christ up onto his cross."

"No Shit?" Terry Whitehead asked, counting again.

"No shit," Anita Martel confirmed counting along with him.

Two months later Samantha Lucas sat alone in a metal chair in silence in the small kitchen eating more tacos. The little room was clean. The windows were open. The junk was gone. The dirt was gone. The old furniture was gone. She sat and chewed another plate of tacos at her elbow. They replaced the linoleum table with an inexpensive plywood pressboard table. Two large plastic tumblers of protein shake sat on the counter behind her, next to folded banana peels and a shiny new blender, still half-full of thick bubbling yellow-white liquid. Its empty cardboard box and packing materials sat on the ground at the end of the counter, with bags of junk, waiting for someone to walk it downstairs to a dumpster out back.

Samantha heard the sound of keys in the lock far below and looked at the clock on her iPhone. Anita Martel walked up the old wooden stairs, kicked off her jock flip-flops, and seated herself in another new cheap metal chair. She scooped a soggy fish taco off the plate and took a large famished bite. She chewed, mouth open, sour cream dripping down her chin from the corner of her mouth.

She wiped at it with a paper napkin from a stack of paper napkins on the table, "Promoter's office called. They set the date.

Confirmed the contender, she's Canadian. She's good. Really fuckin' good."

Samantha Lucas stopped eating, swallowed, smiled, "I'm better. I'm ready. My left feels like steel. I'm faster than ever. I'm on my weight. To the ounce."

She reached behind her and retrieved the protein shakes from the counter, placed one on the table near Anita Martel, drank from the other, long and slow.

She put the tumbler down, smiled, "We made it baby: business is good, I'm in good shape, and you're a phenomenal manager. What could be better?"

Samantha Lucas and Anita Martel lay in bed in the dark talking and smoking.

Anita Martel said, "I never fucking told him. It was none of his business. My ma died when I was so small. My pop, he was so busy teaching me to box, it just never came up. My grandma, I never really talked to her too. Fucking junkie Granny. Overdosed bitch."

Samantha Lucas repeated, "That's fucked up; junkie granny."

Anita Martel said teasing, "Hey granny, I'm headed to the store for a half-dozen eggs and a quart of milk, want me to pick up a dime bag for ya from your dealer on the corner?"

They giggled together, Anita Martel continued, "Hey granny, go give your dealer head and he'll front you a fix!"

They giggled and made fake blowjob and vomit sounds,

Samantha Lucas yelled, "Shut up! I gotta get some sleep."

Anita Martel smiled in the dark, "What time are the painters here tomorrow? Seven?"

Samantha Lucas agreed with her eyes closed, "Yeah, seven, then the lawyers at nine, then we have the new class for the little kids at eleven the photographer at one."

They kissed, Anita Martel said, "Busy day. Good night baby."

Samantha Lucas replied, "Good night."

TKO Anthology

Caught in their kitchens or near their trucks and stands, the eaters of tacos tell their favorite and the makers of tacos explain what makes their tacos the best.

The taco stand taco clerk, taco stand cook in the background smoking, rolled-up magazine in hand, both standing near the painted windows and counter on the sidewalk, "Lingua, we get fresh lingua, boil it, salt it, sauté it in butter. Mmmm."

The Hollywood caterer, in crisp white chef's coat, checked pants, very clean, on the massive sound stage, "We only use the freshest organic ingredients. I make the tofu tacos with Himachi extra firm tofu I marinade in a soy and sesame reduction overnight. Then we wrap them in lard-free, spinach, whole wheat flour tortillas, and top them with pan-roasted sesame seeds."

Bobby McGarry, at a booth inside Taco Time, the stand close to the downtown arena, "I like the ones with beef. The sautéed beef. Carne Asada."

Eddie Holleran, seated across from Bobby McGarry, "Pulled pork. Nothing better than, what'd ya call it? Al pastor? I think it's al pastor."

Officer Tesco, seated at the lunch counter next to her girl friend, just across from Bobby McGarry and Eddie Holleran, "I get a plate of four, two Carne Asada, two al pastor. I used to get a fish taco but it's too messy with the sour cream all over my uniform."

Samantha Lucas, standing near the hospital taco truck, "Fish. I like fish tacos. Pescado. The shrimp are good too, but shrimp are dicey: you get a bad shrimp in a shrimp taco and there are no easy symptoms."

Cindy Roberts, near Samantha Lucas, standing with the hospital taco-truck owner, "I like fried potato. What could be worse for you and better tasting than mashed potatoes in a soft shell fried in, in what?"

Taco truck owner, "lard."

Cindy Roberts, "lard?"

Taco truck owner, smiling, "pork lard."

Cindy Roberts looks ill, "oh my God."

Tres Amigos Muertos chef, in a white chef's coat covered with food, and stained, checked pants, in his sprawling kitchen, "Clarified butter. In five gallon buckets. Enough said."

His souse chefs, tired and hot, smoking and drinking water glasses full of dark cold beer slap him five, they hoot. The dishwashers spraying dish after dish nearby hoot too.

Ted Conway, scowling, seated in the dining room of Tres Amigos Muertos, "I like the crunchy-shell ones. The ones in hard shells. Not those soft shell ones like all the Mexicans eat I'd rather have Italian anytime."

Mark Ellison seated across the small table from Ted Conway, grinning with imagined pleasure, "Al pastor. In soft corn tortillas or rolled tight and pan-fried. Five or six. With beer. Cold yellow Mexican beer."

Anita Martel, sitting alone in her kitchen, "I love Pollo. With cilantro and sour cream and green sauce. Only three or four at a time."

Renata Martinez, Sandy Folson's housekeeper, standing in the kitchen, in front of the massive range, "I make them just like my mama; tripita or chorizo each served on two small corn tortillas with guacamole, salsa, onions, and cilantro. Mmmm so good. The best way to get and keep a man. Good tacos."

Sandy Folson, in her bathrobe, cigarette in hand, sitting across from the housekeeper, "I don't ask, I just eat them. I love them all."

Linda O'Brien, sitting next to Sandy Folson, drink and cigarette in hand, a little Bloody Mary dripped down her zipped brown tracksuit jacket, smiling, "Tripita or lingua. They are hands down the whole point of tacos. A tasty bit of haggis in a warm, soft, corn tortilla."

www.ingramcontent.com/pod-product-compliance
Lightning Source LLC
Chambersburg PA
CBHW020614310726
48979CB00008B/1485/J

* 9 7 8 0 9 8 4 8 9 8 7 2 5 *